ALEXANDER
The Forging of a Warrior President

Written by Amond Williams

Copyright © 2017 Amond Williams
All rights reserved
First Edition

PAGE PUBLISHING, INC.
New York, NY

First originally published by Page Publishing, Inc. 2017

ISBN 978-1-63568-988-4 (Paperback)
ISBN 978-1-63568-989-1 (Digital)

Printed in the United States of America

This book is dedicated to the good people of this world, to the Army, Air force, Marine, Navy, and Coast Guard, to the many military schools which produce such quality soldiers who present maintain an era of somewhat peace in this world, to the men and women who sacrifice have brought great credit and distinction to their countries, governments, families, and friends in this world, and to most of all, to the future youths who are being mentored and molded to maintain and continue a just, and lasting, peace in this world.

CONTENTS

Chapter 1	The World Situation	7
Chapter 2	The Examinations	19
Chapter 3	Academy of the Roughful Military Institute	29
Chapter 4	Going Home	68
Chapter 5	The Island Compound	76
Chapter 6	The Battalion	86
Chapter 7	Protect the President	93
Chapter 8	President Alexander	108
Chapter 9	Aliens Sustain Great Losses	118
Chapter 10	Five Aliens Go Home	122

CHAPTER 1

The World Situation

The year is unknown; the world has stopped monitoring time as in the past centuries; the world society believes that there is no reason anymore. The entire world is now governed and run by a world council made of representatives from every nation in the world. War has been outlawed after the fifth World War, which almost destroyed the entire globe and every living creature on earth, even human existence. After the war, only thirty million humans remained alive and only several species of animals and plants, now the remaining race of people must supervise the rebirth of the world. With the inventions of several modern abilities to travel, communicate, control, and provide for the basic essentials of human existence, the rapid growth and rebuilding seem possible. The two leaders of each thirty-two remaining nations were selected by their people to speak for them in the World Congress. The surviving nations are both crude and modern, and each fate depended on how the last world war affected their country because some nations were sent back into the medieval time while other nations fended quite well. But these distinctions no longer matter because the nations are working to be one now and war was designated as a thing of the past; things are done another way with all receiving equal treatment, and the world resources are now shared fairly.

For centuries, the world has been trying to unify the world nations and countries, and it took a World War to do it. The leaders of the World started to understand if they did not cooperate and coexist, they would not survive the next World War with the world only having thirty million people collectively and war killing twenty million people even during small conflicts. Before World War Five, there were ten billion people on the planet, and now only thirty million people live, and most of them are children. The adults' population is about one six of the world humans (about five million).

In ten years, the world will witness a new and stronger youth population, and the now surviving adults want to instill a more peaceful world without war and nations living together as one. With this in mind, the world leaders have outlawed war and have destroyed or hidden most of the materials of war, including books and anything that reminded people of war, except one school that still prepares leaders for war, and that school is controlled by a very chosen few.

Soon, the only military academy that exists will be closed; experts have predicted in the next fourteen years, it will close forever. The world's humans are struggling for order, unity, and survival, and it looks as if the world is making satisfactory progress. This was the situation or time in which a long-solitary mother will give birth to a male child whose destiny will achieve greatness if it lives. Moreover, in a world that has seen billions die uselessly, it is not surprising that life is not guaranteed.

The scene will be an unknown village somewhere on an island in the Atlantic Ocean, where a nameless rag-tag woman will make a mark on the future of the world's existence by her gift, which she will leave behind. With the nations recovering from war, everyone is fending for themselves until the nations' government work out a world government to take care of the remaining world war survivors. A savior will be born and nurtured. The years of maturing and training of a lone individual from birth to adulthood will make this single event and destiny prediction possible. Helped by the present situation of world affair making what will transpire possible, the birth of a holy one in terms of the warfare. The ancient traditions of past wars and the kindness of humankind will turn this hopeless situation, which comes with a birth of a child, something natural and good. This yet-unborn child surrounded by the blessing to be born and have the chance to be a warrior of unquestionable ability, skills, knowledge, and courage unknown to humanity in any past or present time. Only time can hold or tell the future of humankind and always man have depended on the blessing and care of the creator to provide for continue existence and protection. However, the all-powerful have left clues and signs to foretell its creation destiny; man-made wars have destroyed all evidence of those clues and signs. Ancient forgotten people have foretold of his coming many centuries ago, but a people who have vanished before time. Many times in history, men have hoped for such warrior breaded for fighting and leadership, but all hopes have escaped as only hopeful dreams of impossible hopes. However, at this time and at this moment in time it will come true and the birth of one, which will become such a masterful and gifted leader-warrior, will fulfill the prophecy.

One born of woman and natured by charity and model by a past hero of several past wars, and from the breast of a widow, his benefactor, a mother has been foretold. The true mother walks the lone streets in search of a place to give birth. Nevertheless, the soul of the one in her speaks out to his calling as if fate cannot wait and must share it knowledge to the unborn. Yes, we wait for one unborn, yet, one who will have such courage and bravery, unmatched in human's history. We wait for a story to unfold for all and we must wait patiently for time to work, its magic. The power of fate yells out, one created by mother of bear means and future, lay protected in the womb of the lowest of the lowest. She could not know or think who the father is; she has slept with hundreds or even thousands of men since learning of her situation. The seven to nine months, she has carried what felt to her like the weight of the world and she has carried this burden without help or easy of her status and situation in life. Nevertheless, she knows somehow that her burden is not a burden, but a gift in disguise and she will not be around to enjoy the honor of its purpose. As a mother, she will only want the child to be healthy and not a girl so not to inherit her legacy of life. She prays secretly for a strong baby boy. The hero baby will represent a world being seared by an unknown hoard of men, which is in his life; he will never be told this or much of his origin. The unborn youth visions participation in untold warfare and battles too numerous to comprehend. The unborn youth thinks how this can be possible that he can dream of engaging in wars and battles not yet possible and of his visual images of participation so clearly and define. Is he dead or dying? However, he knows, he is alive and yet not born and waiting preparation and opportunity to come forth. He will be one who has learned at the precious time of coming in the world his need to learn and study all he can of life, military, and warfare. Therefore, in an unknown place and an unknown time, his sole creator has created one to save and protect his creation. Fate will sum up its vision in saying that in the hills and mountains of a forgotten and unknown village is born the future military leader and hero who will lead future troops into a conflicts and battles so unspeakable and hideous that the devil himself will not understand and speak of the insanity of it.

All this is taking place while his mother wanders aimlessly in the streets until she thinks of the only place that she will be welcome. In a village forgotten by men and time, a child who care not of birth or life, rest and sometime moves in the womb of the village bicycle-one who has been rode by most of the males in the village, knocks on the door of the village only saloon. The mother hopes which have two folds: to rid herself of the pain in her womb and to see and hold her new born in her arms. This will be her first child and though she has not figured out how she will feed, clothes, and care for the child. She tells her weaken body and mind to focus on one thing at a time—first birth then life challenges. In her womb, the child who will be the one the world of men will owe their survival and new birth. The door of the saloon finally opens after several, out of control and desperate loud knocks. When Sally opens the salon's door, the battered pregnant woman falls into Sally's arms, and Sally immediately carries the young prostitute in the back room. Sally laid the woman on the bed and asked an old man in the hallway for help. He does not move and sit motionless in the hallway looking in the bedroom because the door to the room was missing. All the other rooms are occupied and because no one wanted a room without a door, the room was emptied. He just sits there and watches. Sally knew that she will be the midwife for this woman which she has seen numerous times but never ask her for her name or exchanged names. The woman is barely clothed for being out in the weather that she has just escaped from and to bear child too. The nameless woman moans in pain foreshadowing the youth role and future status in society and her own doom. The pregnant woman is so weak from lack of nutriment, sleep, and shelter and Sally fear that she will loss both the woman and the child. Sally knew from years of being a midwife that the mother cannot be saved and there is a slime hope for the baby to survive. However, Sally is an experience midwife and she had brought hundreds of babies in this world and as an assistant nurse, she had seen hundreds of young and old adults leave this world, which have fought and died in the wars. However, after several hours of touch and go, an echo of a baby cry just once filled the room, hallway, saloon, and outside signaling a new birth, the mother reaches for her baby. The strength the mother used to extend her arms to hold her child will be the last thing she would do in this life. Her arms fall and she is dead, but she died with a simile of joy in her face and eyes to see that her baby was a healthy boy.

Yet, some might say our story begins with the birth of the child; we who looks farther would say our story begins with the chance of human survival at the graceful sacrifice of the life of a strong and loving mother. Sally holds the baby and looks at a brave and strong mother who was weak from lack of nutriment and broken by years of improper care, past from life fighting for the life of her child and won the fight. Though the lord of darkness claimed a prize, he did not get her baby, too. Sally smiled to know the woman did live long enough to see her baby boy, but she is dead now. She fought and struggled to save her baby and deserved a more fitting burial than the one, which awaits her. The old man who watched the several hours struggle for life against death, finally gets up to take the dead mother's body outside for the morning death patrol to claim the body and to take their cargo to the burning ditch outside of town to be cremated with several other unknown people's bodies. On the heap of bodies lay the dead mother now considered nothing more than a creature whose end story ended in a room in a salon which she visited many times to earn her keep and survival, only hours ago its locality provided the shelter for the birth of her first and last baby and her death place. With the body of the mother gone, Sally knew what to do with the dead mother's newborn since she could not care for a small child.

A shadow fall on the dead mother's body on the pile of dead, so what, the chance of receiving last rite, an impossible chance, though the cremation ditches were somewhat near the village only church. The ministers (pastors, bishops, et al.) which provided service for the people of the village would sometimes, long ago, come out of the warmth and comfort of the church and say a few words before the cremations, but this seldom happens now because the dead here cannot pay for their services. They believed that their time is best served blessing the dead of ones who family, friends, or relatives who can offer or leave a sizable sum of money for their services or time. The burners pour a sizable mixture of whale oil and an unknown substance found in the barrels, which years ago washed up on the shores of their small village. The mixture has proven satisfactory for thousands of cremations in the past and again the mixture will prove successful again. The dead bodies disappear in the flames and so the earthly body of the future warrior-leader's mother is consumed along with the other bodies and so the mother's earthly body will leave without having a proper ceremony and thus destroying any chance of securing hope of social memory. She is gone from the thoughts of men.

Now the time of the lone nude youth birth has come to pass and his stay and existence stands in the balance of the next few unpredictable hours of actions of Sally (the lone midwife). Sally, an old woman, wraps the newborn child in an old discarded blanket, which was used to cover the horses and mules in the salon's stable. The grossly smelly blanket is large enough to wrap the entire baby and protect the baby from the cold and wind and gives a reasonable amount of warmth during the journey, which Sally and the baby will be force to make this rainy, cold, windy, dark, and lonely night. In anticipation, the newborn baby boy does not cry, but shows a vigor burst of energy for the pending ordeal or peril of unnatural sense. Sally looks at the baby's reaction with a glaze and wonderment, but turn quickly to focus on the tasks. Sally dressed herself as warm as possible, held the baby in the roll of the discarded wool blanket as firmed as possible, and opened the salon's door. Outside is rainy and cold. The wind is blowing hard and steady, but Sally is able to drive herself and her valuable packet or cargo to the winding road that lead to their destination. As if faith drove Sally, as it drove the birth mother, Sally drives to accomplish her hard and difficult task as if it was a mission, which could not risk failure as if failure was not an option. The mission had to be completed at all cost and the survive of this little one was foretold as in the past things were foretold and predicted in the scrolls found many thousands of centuries ago by man. Sally will fall several times before she arrives at her destination. Therefore, as she took the baby north on the road, the wind and element fought her efforts and lost. Nature tried hard to break her will power, but Sally is a strong willed woman birthed during conflicts, matured by years of wars, and tested by the will, which only the strong have and thus have survived. Survival being just an unpleasant fact to her, Sally maintains her pace and plows through the heavy down pour of rain and the strong force of the wind. The baby boy is in the angel like hands of a true survivalist. Finally, Sally makes it to the door of a lone mansion size home on the out shirt of the village. She carefully lowers the child down on the steps of the pouch and knocks hard on the thick wooden door and listen closely for a noise of the occupant coming to tend to the door. When Sally heard the slights but audio able sound, she quickly left the baby alone and started back to the salon, knowing that she has done the right thing, and that the baby would be in good loving hands. She vanishes in the rain and the darkness of the night.

The door opens, and the elder woman looks for an adult or adults, either male or female or both, but finds neither and is about to close the door when she looks down. For the first time, she sees the gift that will bring years of delight to her lonely life and happiness to her household. To see a wonderful gift is beyond her imagination and now staring straight at her with open and penetrating eyes and reaching with his tiny hands suggesting to her to pull him carefully into the bosom of his future mother and benefactor. The elder woman fears that a careful look around for the baby's mother, father, or parents would bring this blessing to an abrupt end and, thus she does not waste time in picking up the child and closing the large wooden door. The child curls up lovingly in the woman's arms; the woman whose name is Mary, a fitting and proper name for this savor, a child, which will someday lead a worldly armed force of untold numbers against a potentially unbeatable force.

The child will be well taken care of and nurtured by Mary. Mary is a widow of an old gent who fought in World War Three, Four, and Five. Her husband, Colonel John, had been awarded numerous times and twice awarded the nation's highest "Medal of Honor" for extreme bravery in the face of several enemy attacks and assaults of superior forces and power. The last event that earned her husband his second "Medal of Honor" took his life, but his life was not lost in vein, because of his actions, he saved hundreds of thousands of men and women's lives and ended the last World War (World War Five). Both the victors and the losers honored him as a hero and a man who sacrifice lead to a globe realization that the world cannot afford to lose such men and women of his character. Colonel John was a vital part of bring the world-to-world peace and his death will not be the end of his efforts to save the world and provide peace, harmony, and humanity.

Colonel John will become an important factor in rising of the child. Mary will name her adopted baby boy Alexander and raise him as Colonel John would have raised Alexander if he was alive. He would be homed school and trained by Mary. She will teach him everything Colonel John had known about war and warfare. Colonel John had won several major campaigns and numerous battles. He had turned down several field promotions to general and General of All fighting forces of his nation's Army, but he turned the promotions down to live and fight with the troops. As a general, General John would have been safe from the front and harm. Alexander marbled at the stories, which Mary told him of his stepfather turning down safety and position to be a true warrior. Alexander thought silently that he would follow the heroic steps of the late Colonel John (his Father) as described by Mary (his Mother). As soon as Alexander was able to learn, Mary started his homeschooling and military training.

ALEXANDER

Alexander was a natural at learning and his ability to read and comprehend material was just amazing and he commanded an abnormal memory capacity. He, by his mother, will be instructed on several languages, West Civilization, World History, World Government, World Geography, World Economics, Government, Economics, Psychology, Sociology, Science, Mathematics, and the Art of War. He received so many other classes and by his seventh birthday, he had received excellent marks in all his classes. As a result, Mary tried hard to encourage Alexander at seven years old to go to Academy Preparation School so he would easily pass the requirements and tests for the best Military School when he reaches the age of ten. Very few boys would pass the difficult tests, both physical and mental requirements to enter the Academy of Roughful Military Institute. Her husband Colonel John had founded the school when he was a lieutenant, during the Third World War to train and provided the best military leaders the country could train to leave the country men and women into combat and ensure a decisive victory with minimum losses in human casualties, equipment, and materials in the numerous battles of the third World War. Since Alexander was named after a great past warrior leader, Mary pushed Alexander. And at the age of seven, Mary required Alexander to work out three times a day, with addition, to run one mile in the morning, one mile at noon, and one mile before bed without question. It did not matter how hard the day had been or how bad the weather, Alexander accomplished the tasks required by Mary. Mary's motto was trained hard in peace and bleed less in war. He was also required to do unspoken numbers of push up, sit up, and several other extreme exercises to prepare for the harshness and extreme environment of continue warfare and the demands of war and its battles. Mary loved Alexander, and Alexander loved his Mother and he never complained about his training and the method he received it. Alexander was a natural born soldier and Mary and he knew it. It was all about trust and he would always trust his Mother.

Alexander was always energetic and ready for the day and what it had to bring and with his unpredictable mother controlling the events of the day. He expected nothing short of rough and uncompromised challenges and adventure. He would expect no less from his dear mother and his mother never let him down; training was always hard and demanding. After a while, Alexander sensed that he had an innate ability and was equipped with a secret weapon: his endless energetic energy, his incanted ability to learn quickly and completely, and his ability to translate his ability into action and he was a charismatic leader. He grew strong and intelligent which has always been a hallmark, necessarily of a great leader. His military training and schooling would last all day and seven days a week and Alexander would love the program and the time he spent with his mother and that include time in the world of his father. His mother will continually remind him that learning and training will make him a man, worthy of the title of being call a man. Mary had all day and part of the night to make him appreciate life and his destiny.

When Alexander turned eight, Mary showed him the Colonel's Library and study, which made everything before the Colonel's Library schooling seem trivial or mediocre. Colonel John was one of the few men in the world who were authorized to retain books, manuscripts, and materials on warfare. The Colonel's library will be Alexander real teaching source. The library was well organized, but when Alexander and his mother started home schooling in the library, the library became a mess with books everywhere and several books laid open—open books laid for Alexander to read and absorb the information stored in the special and crucial pages of each open book. Manuscripts of Colonel John's documented lessons learned from mistakes in open warfare, to battles won, and to battles loss. Colonel John had stored information so if the peace of the day ended; true leaders with good intentions and motives could rise up warring forces, win, and return the world power to a normal peace. From reading Colonel John's manuscripts, Alexander learned something surprising and hard to believe that Colonel John hated warfare and its hideous result or aftermath and he only fought earnestly to end the horrors created by warfare. Alexander noted this information and understood a peaceful solution should be sorted out before the dogs of hell should be releases, in the form of an all-out war.

ALEXANDER

Alexander read hundreds of books on military leadership, battle strategies, logistic, battle staffing, map reading, cost and expend ages or usages of supplies, man power, and battle field analyzes, intelligent gathering on the enemy, and ways to use intelligent to your advantage, etc. He would stay long hours in the Colonel John's library even after Mary had said that learning was over for the day. Mary did not mind his dedication and devotion to learning all he could learn because well-trained leaders end war and bring a long era of peace. Nevertheless, as every mother, she hopes that Alexander would never have to experience war or fighting. Though she was training, her son to be a warrior, she could not imagine how well, she could take losing another person that she truly loved and care for.

As Alexander grew older and wiser, Mary and Alexander always found the time to be mother and child in a normal worldly way. It made their life happy and fulfilling. They would enjoy looking at the moon, the stars, and the planets together, and reading books, picnics, all types of games and many more activities. Mary sang numerous songs to Alexander which he learned most of them and sometime they both sang together as a duet. They knew that they would never be famous as singer, but they sang any way. He was always kind and helpful with Mary and he made it understood that she was his mother and Colonel John was his father and it will be that way always. As mother and son aged, their love only grew stronger and an unbreakable bond was formed and forged. The bond between a mother and son was created and forged from the first day, Mary and a small baby met on a cold, stormy rainy, and windy night several years ago. Mary's son Alexander was her pride and joy.

The manor where they live were somewhat in the countryside and other than the two faithful and dedicated servants who managed the manor and assist in the manor upkeep, Mary received very few visitors. Alexander found time in his busy schedule to help with the upkeep and work around the yard and in the family's house. He would work long hours on the manor's garden, grounds, sweeping floors, cleaning walls, washing dishes, and any things that he saw and could understand needed doing. The two housekeepers and workers loved him and he loved them (Martha and Mattie). To Alexander,

Martha and Mattie were his family, too. They were great people and they lived, and worked on the manor. They were part of the family that Colonel John and Mary had adopted many years ago. Time was passing and Mary wanted Alexander to attend the Military School that her husband found when he was just a Lieutenant. in the country's army. Alexander was soon to be ten and it was time to pass the tests and mental examinations to win a place at the famous military school (which was consider the best in the world and the hardest school to get admission) and family position and status could not get you entrance. You had to pass the grueling "Spartan Entrant Examinations" or die trying.

 The initial testing and examinations to enter and compete for entrant to Roughful Military Academy Institute require the potential candidates to leave their homes alone without family or support. Alexander woke early the morning of the entrance test to the dangerous and grueling "Spartan Entrant Examination." Mary, Martha, and Mattie will stay at home and the hired driver who occasionally drove for the family will take Alexander to the train station. Alexander arrives thirty minutes early to the train station and has plenty of time to check in and receive his train ticket to the unknown testing location. The driver made sure that Alexander boarded the train and he watched the train disappear from sight before he left the train station. Alexander watches anxiously out of the train's window trying to anticipate his destination and symbolically be the master of his future. It is said that if one knows where one is going the person has some control of their future. Alexander slowly drifts to sleep and after several hours, he wakes. The train slowly comes to a stop and Alexander has reached his destination.

CHAPTER 2

The Examinations

The Spartan Entrant Examinations was the hardest examinations on the globe to pass and out of the about thirty-two nations in the world on an average of about thirty million total population and a little less than five millions eligible to enter only about one out of hundreds of thousands have passed the initial application to complete the final examinations. Very few ten-year-old boys wanted to try out for the school and every year, the school had been having problems in recruitment, especially since the school would not even think about lowering its entrance requirements. The globe society changed a few rules to make up and fill the places of the ones that pass the tests and fail the physical, but that rule change might have only lead to the unfortunate youth's demise. The test last for several days, without schedule breaks, minimum rest periods, time to eat, time to sleep, and other function at your own risk, the last day is a grueling test of physical strength, endurance, and combative skills that could easily break an adult male. Young children will take this test and there have always been cases in the pass and will by design, children will be completely exhausted by the examination extreme requirements. It was a test that was unforgiving and extremely mentally stressful and on the form of the application, it had in large letters that the weak and weak of heart do not apply. Alexander is now ten years old and his time to try to get admitted to the Academy of Roughful Military Institute has arrived. When Alexander asked his mother if he was ready before he left home, Mary told Alexander that he was ready and she felt that he will do quite well because he is adequately prepared. Alexander knew that he must face the initial examinations alone and it was up to him, now. Alexander filled out the application, took the initial examinations, and passed. Alexander was amongst the very few to try out for the main examinations to entrance to enter the famous Academy of Roughful Military Institute and pass. The first day of the world examinations (the Spartan Entrant Examinations) will be tomorrow and it were hard for Alexander to sleep waiting in participation of the competition and challenges which would be facing him. The morning of the testing finally came.

There were two thousand boys at the test field and there were hundreds of lines to pick up their seal test packages, which weighed about a hundred pound. The events were set up that there were a test monitor for each examinee to ensure examinees did not cheat or to enforce the rules. The punishment for cheating or getting help of any kind was immediate execution to be carried out immediately by your monitor who visually carried on his hip, a holster that held a 500 caliber block buster, which became famous because it could easily penetrate forty inches of steel. At one time in history, it took a rocket launcher or missile to penetrate forty inches of steel. No one was allowed in the testing area except the ones being tested and any violators of this would be immediate shot with the 500 caliber blockbuster carried by your monitor who was awarded several thousands of dollars each time he had the opportunity to use his blockbuster. Several years ago, several monitors were found guilty of discharging their blockbusters to get the money, but now there is an eye in the sky to watch the monitors. Each hundred thousands of youths killed by the monitors have been justified by the eye in the sky. The eye in the sky has been tested to be a hundred percent reliable. Alexander took his package to his test site and when the bell rung he opened, his package and started the test. He picked up his test package at three in the morning, and the bell rang at five that morning. The test or examination was extremely long and difficult and Alexander felt that some of the examinees were not prepare for the examinations, but Alexander felt good about his test performance. All during the testing, he could hear the thundering roar of the 500 caliber blockbusters dealing out final and permanent justice to cheaters and violators. At the beginning of the examination, Alexander estimated that every thirty minutes, he heard a blockbuster end the life of a test violators. Alexander worked on his examination and finished the next day at noon. During the night, Alexander heard the loud sound of the famous blockbuster every hour by morning the two thousands were down to five hundred. Alexander while going to turn in his test was sprayed with blood and bones of the brains of a youth. Alexander was relieved to be finished with the test, especially since his monitor was getting itchy and pulled out his gun several time scream the words, "You cheating Bitch." After he turned in his test, he had a five hours and a half break to prepare for the other examination phase. Alexander had heard from Mary and others the second phase was even more deadly than the first phase and the phases got harder as the testing progressed. The monitors were given the names of the examinees who have failed the examination and their monitors killed them immediately. When the next day came only about two hundred of the two thousands tested lived or survived the lethal monitors and their deadly 500 caliber blockbusters.

When the bell rung a second time, it signaled the end of the first phase of the grueling and deadly testing required to gain admission to the world's most famous Academy of Roughful Military Institute. The boys were exhausted, but they were looking forward to taste the victory of passing the world's toughest military entrance examinations and attending the famous elite military training program. Helicopters brought in a special group of test monitors and again each examinee had a monitor, but this time they were outfitted with an 800 caliber Widow Maker sniper rifles with a high technical scopes which gave the expert users a 99.9 killing accurate ratio up to five miles. The Widow Maker earned its name in the last desert war and became a battle changer and the units who command the most Widow Makers usually were ensured victory. Alexander noticed that each monitor had an abnormal large firing eye, which was problematical deformed by many years shooting or firing his assigned weapon, the 800 caliber Widow Maker. Players were told that the monitors were instructed to shoot and kill anyone who diverted one meter off the training course, tried to cheat, was injured, and any one not finishing the course after an undisclosed number of examinees finished the course.

Only thirty-two ten-year-old boys will be alive from the original number of two thousand entrants when the course number is met. The examinations were built in phases to continue until the thirty-two cadets' number was met. Tournament so to speak: the second phase was a 26 miles plus marathon with rolling hills and several hills to be done in an unknown time limit as expedited as possible was what the briefer mentioned and he added slacker will be shot. The monitors knew and the examinees knew that the farthest distance monitors will be from the examinees would be less than two hundred feet, an easy kill for an expert 800 caliber Widow Maker sniper. Each monitor sat next to their target smiling when the briefer mentioned their duties and responsibility on when to eliminate their assigned target (examinee). After the briefing, they were informed that they had five minutes to prepare for the marathon. The remaining candidates pulled up their socks, tighten their shoelaces, and drunk plenty of water. Alexander hydrated all day and night before this event and ate some good many high calorie meals to give him, strength and endurance during the event. They lined up and the canons signal, with a thunderous roar, the start of the marathon.

Alexander started slow and steady as several other ten-year-old boys did. Their monitors followed closely on their Advanced Mighty Max Four Wheelers with the sniper rifles in their pouches. This event should have been an easy task or trial for the boys, but only after seven miles, the first distinguish sound of the 800 caliber Widow Maker was heard. The first child had stop to relieve himself and accidently was about less than an inch off the course; he would not have to worry about any more bodily function anymore. The monitor paraded the kill or body for the entire group to see how the 800 caliber Widow Maker sniper rifle can take a head clean off and sear the blood veins and arteries without leaving not a single blood spray or stain on the victim's clothes. Alexander thought the monitor was a sick person and quickly rememorized his face for future recognition.

ALEXANDER

At thirteen miles, about twenty-five boys were dead for one reason or another. Alexander was still feeling good and continue his pace and conserved his strength for the three huge hills: Agony, Misery, and Heartbreak. About fifteen miles out, Alexander started negotiating Agony, he took it easy and paced himself, and after the first hill, he was still feeling good. And about twenty miles out, Alexander started feeling the need for water, but he knew that he was still fine. He kept his pace and finish running up Misery, but he knew like the other boys the last and most difficult hill was Heart Break. He passed several boys who had muscle cramps or heat exhaustion. All the boys were victims of their monitors' 800 caliber Widow Makers. At around twenty-five out, about quarter of a mile, Alexander could see several boys running the last leg of the marathon, Heart Break Hill. When Alexander reached the base or foot of the hill, he was still feeling good and maintained a steady and deliberate pace. At the top of Heart Break, he could see the finish line at the base. He knew that the run down would be easy, but any slip could result in a sprain or a broken leg and end in a sudden death by the report of the 800 caliber Widow Maker sniper rifle his monitor kept closely at his side. Alexander made it to the finish line and started hydrating and eating for the next event.

The starting two hundred were down to one hundred and twenty-one. The next event was the jungle navigation trials. Alexander and the other ten-year-olds were flown over several hours to an area somewhere in Africa. Several small planes landed in the arena bring in a new briefer and one hundred and twenty-one new monitors. The monitors were equipped with the Advanced Strong Armed Bow, which became famous in the Fourth World War and used primary as an assassin weapon for silence kills behind enemy lines, one of the Black Operation forces most lethal and well-used weapon of death. The monitors were lean and in excellent condition and wore badges of "Bow Expert Extreme" which only a few in the world could obtain the knowledge and skills to earn. They also proudly wore a patch illustrating or advertising they were jungle experts. Alexander had no doubt of their skills and proficient with their weapons. The briefer informed the participates that the requirements were to travel ten miles in triple canopy jungle in five to eight hours without getting lost or making contact with the villagers or people living in the jungle area if any of these restrictions are violated their monitors will do their duties and responsibility and take you out. He ended his briefing with saying, "Are there any questions? No questions? You have thirty minutes." Alexander and many others reviewed their maps and tracing their route by avoiding paths and areas which will lead to a village or area known to draw humans as a clearance, water sources, known map routes, paths, hill-tops, farm areas, etc. Alexander will take the side of ridges, side of hills, and bottoms, which were infected with snakes and alligators. Thirty minutes was up.

The group of navigators along with their angel of death (monitors) headed into the abyss of the jungle. Alexander immediately took the low ground which made traveling difficult especially in triple canopy, but Alexander knew that he must move fast before darkness came and then the jungle beneath the canopy will be totally black and movement would be slow or almost impossible. Alexander started moving with a pace that even his physical fit monitor lagged somewhat. He was making good time and within three hours, he had travel six miles of the ten miles, but visibility was getting difficult and instead of slowing down, Alexander speeded up which surprise his deadly monitor. Alexander only slowed down when he was within two miles of the finishing point to check his map. Since it was almost completely dark, he knew to avoid areas where light because it would be a prime place for people because people like light to see. Therefore, the last two miles to the finish line, travel was in complete darkness, but Alexander made it, ok.

After the jungle events, facts of examinees being killed by animals and several examinees had to be brought down because they were biting by poison snakes. Alexander had survived several phases and had stayed alive and he ensured himself that carelessness and confidence could be his biggest and most deadly enemy. He must maintain a thinking process to survive.

When the event was over, Alexander was still full of energy and he waited anticipating on what the next phase of testing would be. There were just one hundred boys left. The examinees and Alexander were flown to an island in South America. The new monitors were old warriors and resemble, the ancient navy seals. They were not a blood thirsty group as the previous monitors; they were the best at their jobs and took pride in their job performance. They were just as deadly as their predecessors were, with only one hundred boys remaining alive; the odds on surviving had dropped sharply. The monitors boarded their speed boats armed with a strange canon. We will find out soon what those canons were. The boys and Alexander were told to board several waiting helicopters and they flew for several hour and touch down early that day on a shore where groups of boats laid half out of the water. The navy seal like team were in place to carry out their monitor missions; they had sailed their boats while we flew on helicopters to our starting point. A new briefer faced the boys and said, "We are to be sent out in a group of five and the boats that we will use can safely hold only four people. You are a team recovering a somewhat heavy treasure chest on a small island designated on your map and you are to return from the island with all your team members and the treasure chest. Your monitors would be following you in special war crafts with 40 mm canons, which they are, order to destroy the team who lose a member of their team or do not finish their missions by noon. Your teams are already picked. You have one minute to cast off to your mission, or your team will be shot by an elite special sniper group located somewhere in this area overlooking their target you. Go!"

Alexander was designated as the leader of his team and immediately he commanded to do the map work and assign responsibility in the water to eliminating the possible of being late for cast off and the team killed before any chance to complete the mission. Alexander was the first in the water and boat and told one of the team member to hold on the back of the boat (where normally a motor would be attached the stern). He informed the team that they would take turns every hour to hold on the back (stern) of the boat. Then, he directed them to paddle in sequence, and he initiated reading the map, plotted a course at fifty-two degrees for two hours and ninety degrees for one hour, and had two boys who said that they were experience water navigators to check his computation. There was no room for error. When the course was confirmed, Alexander's group rowed at a steady pace. Then Alexander set up a chain of command and they worked out a plan what to do if all members needed to be in the boat. When Alexander got in the water, they were one hour to their island and all was well. Several time Alexander heard in the distance the loud sound of the 40 mm canon. They retrieved the chest and was on their away to the finish line when their navy war boat armed with the 40mm canon started directing their main crew 40 mm canon toward them. A group of hunger hammerheads wanted an easy ready to eat meal of one of their team member in the water for lunch, but Alexander emergency immediate reaction plan went in to action. The stern boy was position-laying length wide on the laps of the paddlers with the somewhat heavy treasure chest in the middle of his back, which he did not complain. He figured that he would rather prefer a little pain than be the meals for the hammer head sharks or hear the 40 mm canon kill the team and him. The boat sunk slightly but the movement and rate of travel of the boat was not affected much. Alexander's team arrived safe and on time. One team member was not destroyed by a monitor, but he met his faith by being stung by several jelly fish. Though he was in great pain from the attack of the jelly fish stings, he survived long enough for his team to finish the test. Unfortunately, hours after the event, the young heroic team member died from the numerous stings and shock. Only sixty-four boys survived this event. It was a perfect number for the last event to retain the required thirty-two finishers. The boys and Alexander were flown to Las Vegas for the final test. All the famous people, important people, rich people, and politicians were there to watch the fight to the death to become a student of the most famous Academy of Roughful Military Institute. The last and final event will be a fight to the death. At this event, there were no monitors, but there were many important nations' leaders. The boys were pair by sizes and weight and told that they will fight to the death and the winner will be admitted to the school. Several fights took place before Alexander's battle. When it came to Alexander fight, Alexander was mentally ready and he remember reading in Colonel John's notes that the fight does not always goes to the better fighter, but the one who stay in the fight. His opponent had a black belt in several martial arts and the onlookers had already selected the winner. However, they had under estimated the destiny, cunning, and fight of a boy with a lion's heart and a will to overcome every obstacle life has thrown at him. He was destined to survive and lead. The boy name was Neal, he was confidence of an easy victory, and when Alexander entered the ring, Neal laughed at his adversary. However, if we can remember several centuries ago about a man name Abe Lincoln and the enormous strength that he processed, we would not so eagerly give up on Alexander's survival chances. When the horn blew, Neal came out with a high kick, which nearly took Alexander's head off. Alexander straggled back and was close to losing conscious, but instead of finishing Alexander, Neal made a fatal mistake and danced around the ring to taut his prey when Neal came in for the kill by throwing a deathblow at Alexander. Alexander caught Neal's fist and brought him to the floor. Alexander began to hammer fist, Neal like a mad man until Neal's body laid taunt and still on the canvas. Alexander had proved to himself that when he receives the call to kill; he will not take it lying down, but do what a soldier must do. This was probably what this test was all about. The crowd was stung by the sear brute of Alexander's win. As the man that killed Macbeth in one of Shakespeare's play, Alexander too, have been untimely ripped from the womb of his dying birth mother several years early. In addition, the not so distance future, Alexander will hold several degrees in black belts of the most deadly hand-to-hand combative martial art combat in the known world. Finally, the competition was over and thirty-two ten-year-old boys stood strong; they all were bloody and injured, but they were alive and had won an entrance to the Academy of Roughful Military Institute (the best military school in the known world).

The boys did not receive a ceremony for their accomplishment, because in the past celebration had created leaders who valued awards and decorations instead of self-satisfaction and honor in one's country to serve and if die, their death will be for the greater good, for the survival of your country and its way of life and nothing else or more. Their legacy will be remembered as a person of great character and personal worth to their fellow man, their nation, and the world. Alexander knew why only thirty-two could live and the rest had to die. The world had found out centuries ago that you must either retain the greater devotions of a special and skillful few and eliminate the rest because the rest became the dictators and problems of the world. The children that were killed if they had lived their ambitions for military conquest and power would have developed out of controlled many years later just as the warlords of Africa, Hitler of Nazi Germany and the Stalin of Soviet Union had proven many centuries ago. The wisdom of this thinking seems cruel, but it has proven true for so many centuries. After experiencing several world wars, the world could have identified these warrior leaders at an early age, and ended their life. The era of man could have been spared the agonies of many wars if the world had limited and control the destiny of these warmonger leaders and made them honorable and peaceful leaders. What Colonel John's secret manuscripts informed Alexander of was to honor a lasting and sacred peace at almost any cost but be willing if need be, give the utmost sacrifice (your life) for your convictions as Colonel John did and any real military leader and soldier will do.

Alexander will be able to go home for a few days to recuperate and say, "good-by to love ones." Mary was happy to see and know that Alexander was alive and successfully made the Military Academy. The thirty-two remaining nations had a special day celebration for the successful efforts of the survivors and on the same day celebration to mourn the death of the brave children who quest for excellent fell short of their world's expectations. However, those days, Mary used them to heal Alexander's wounds as she had done for her husband (Colonel John). She told Alexander that a soldier must lick his wounds and prepare for the next battles. He cannot enjoy himself, until the objective or mission is completed and she ensured him, his destiny will be completed.

CHAPTER 3

Academy of the Roughful Military Institute

Time at home with Mary went fast. The morning of Alexander's departure for school or the military school was different. They both woke up early, but they did not speak to each other, yet they distinctively watch each other every move. The military school will not challenge Alexander in a life and death match or situation as the examinations did, but it had its danger. Mary and Alexander will be apart for four years. Alexander is not a Mama's boy, but he has grown close to his mother like a best friend. Alexander will be fourteen the next time; he sees his Mother Mary. Again, Mary will be lonely as she was before Alexander came into her life, one windy, rainy, and cold morning. Although she knew, he will be back it still hurt. Alexander had learned to be hard and seem as if the departure was nothing more than a regular event in one's life, but deep in Alexander's heart, he also hurt. Without a word between the two, they ate breakfast. The car was brought around to take Alexander to the train station. Mary told the driver that she will drive today and to take the day off. Alexander loaded his one small bag into the car and they drove off. Mary drove off abnormally slow in an attempt to get as much time as she could with her son before he was off to military school. His mother looked at Alexander, and Alexander looked at Mary and all they needed to say was said. They had secured an unbreakable bond that separation could not destroy. Finally, she pulled up to the train station, he checked in, and Mary and Alexander waited patiently for the 9:40 a.m. train. And after an hour, they both could hear the train thundering in the distance and within minutes, it was pulling in the station for a ten-minute stop, unload, load up, and go. Alexander finally broke the silence and hugged his mother and softly said, "Good-by" and said that he will miss her." She replied that she will miss him and that she was proud of him.

Alexander did not look back because he knew that he would be back home in four years and Mary, Mattie, and Martha will be home to greet his return. Therefore, he focused on his future and what challenges it will bring. Several other future cadets were on the train and Alexander and they spoke carefully of the ordeals of the examination. Soon they were asleep and enjoying the rolling coaster ride of the train movement. The train ride for them last several hours, stopping and starting to add riders and lose riders. In addition, the cadets knew because of the world situations and governing body this will be the last class of cadets going to the Academy of Roughful Military Institute. Congress of the World have seen no use of producing military leaders in a world which have banded war and anything closed to fighting forever. The Congress of the World was not aware that the future might bring no other option or alternative than to fight. The route going to the train station where the cadets will get off along with other cadets follow a path of turns, curves, hills, mountains, stops, starts, and straight a ways were a small foreshadowing of their future life and military challenges and successes. If Alexander would only had known his route to his sole and Godly existence would be so rough and demanding. He would have possibly braced himself against the very seat; he was sitting in by digging his fingers in the bottom of the seat and forcing his butt and back hard against the seat. This act would be a rebellious reaction to his future decisions, which will be the cause of many lives of both the defenders and aggressors to cease to exist. He will be truly proud of his awesome trained army of men, women, and children, a force not seen in the course of world history or time ready to engage in a struggle of total survival of the fitness and the strongest of will and purpose. A force birth only once to ensure the survival of the race of men and democracy, he will command and nurture without thought but instinctively. He has prepared for this all his life; he was birth to this position, job, and command. With a motto Failure Is No Option and hope that he must overcome if we are to survive. Suddenly, Alexander woke and his dream or nightmare was gone. And as suddenly as he woke up, Alexander was again asleep; Alexander had drifted back in time to give honor and respect to Mary's husband, Colonel John and add to his legacy of achievements, for even in death his adoptive dead father, Colonel John had produced a son in his own image. Moreover, Colonel John though his widow, books, notes, and manuscripts had prepared Alexander for the most prestigious military academy in the world or in which the world had ever known. The only dad that he will only know had produced in him undying respect for him and his achievements and his present in his life. Mary had made this possible because she believed that Alexander needed a father figure in his life and what better man than her loving husband, Colonel John. Alexander braced for a legacy of his own fitting and proper for a son of Colonel John and his mother Mary. His thoughts of the thousands of pages of books and manuscripts that he had read and studied and the hours of exercises and work, Mary required of him since the age of five and how he enjoyed every minutes, hours, and days of it. The single fact of destiny and ambitious efforts will make his destiny someday a fact in its self. Soon Alexander was in a deep sleep and his mind and space of perceptions and thoughts were completely dark and blank. He will sleep well and rejuvenated his mind and his body.

Finally, after several hours, the train stopped at their destination a lone station seldom used and only purpose was to let off the Academy of Roughful Military Institute cadets for school and military training, which only happen once a year. This will be the last four years. Alexander instinctually woke up several minute before arriving at the train station. He was ready for the initial greeting or shock of being at the train station and being pick up by a famous cadre of the school. Colonel John had mentioned several time in his manuscripts and books proudly pointing out his loyalty, devotion, and military abilities. The large figure of an old sergeant stood alone in the distance and said nothing to the cadets; they knew instinctively to fall in formation in front of him at attention (you could hear a pen drop). In addition, he said nothing after what seem several hours after all the cadets assembled in front of him in proper formation. He gave a loud commanding orders to face right and march. The cadets started marching (not saying a word) and they marched for about ten miles. All during the march, it rained, lightening, and the wind blew wildly and cadets march the ten miles in silence. Cadets and Alexander stopped in front of a huge gate and a sign read that the Academy of Roughful Military Institute gate will open at four o'clock in the morning. It was nine o'clock. The old sergeant gave the ordered to fall out and that cadets will assemble again at four o'clock tomorrow, at four o'clock standard time. While several cadets stood motionless, Alexander like several others teamed up and started camp. Alexander and his group left formation to find a place to set up and build temporary living quarters to stay dry. Alexander watched the old sergeant quickly set up a make shift shelter and within minutes Alexander could smell the food and coffee. Alexander and several boys' bed down together after fixing a suitable shelter and they talked openly about the use of time because time was banded or the use of time was banded. The Congress of the World Leaders had banned the use of time. The cadets were not questioning the right and wrong of the Academy of Roughful Military Institute methods and doctrine of the use of time but how will it be used in their training. The school was the best in the world and produced the best and brightness military officers in the Globe (World) and their methods had been tried and true and have become war doctrine on many of world battlefields throughout the planet. One of the members looked out of their shelter and the sign had been taken down and another one hanged professionally in its place and read, "We will make you the best military officer and leader in the world or break you trying." The cadets stood almost motionless for a few moments looking at the sign. It gave a nerving affect, but they had been harden by years of training and preparations to pass the academy's examinations so it was only happy news that their comrades did not die in vain and their will to survive and effort and hard work would paid off. Although the other cadets were in a different frame of mind than Alexander, they were all capable youths of unusual skills and abilities. They would not be here if they were not the best in some form, shape, and manner. Given time, they will overcome many natural and unnatural obstacles of their past and future ordeal; it was born in their nature and strengthened by their uncanny will power. Most of the strengths of the cadets' ability have been proven by the completion of the trials to enter the Academy of Roughful Military Institute. About an hour, the encampment was silent; everyone was asleep and enjoying the music of the rain and wind.

After a hard grueling night, the old sergeant yelled for the cadets to form up since we did not have what we will later be given and learn to tell time—a wind up timepieces that the old sergeant called a watch. About the time, cadets were all in the formation the huge gates of the Military School were open. All around the camp or compound was signs to motive cadets, but the one Alexander took at heart was, "Failure is no option." This sign will always be Alexander's favor. Moreover, surprising to us, the old sergeant introduced himself to us. He said that his name was Sergeant Will and we will address him as Sergeant Will and he will address us as cadets or your cadets' positions, i.e. cadet commander, cadet sergeant major, first cadet, or second cadet, etc. We could tell that Sergeant Will had seen and participated in many battles from the numerous scars on his face and arms. He had a rough and harsh voice that somehow demanded our immediate obedience and trust. He only told us once and we reacted immediately. During this transition and indoctrination, Alexander and several friends that he had met at the "Examination" and during the long night camp out assisted the military institute cadre in organizing the other cadets for outfits. There were lines for everything the cadets would need to complete the school and everything a soldier and a student could imagine were given to the students during this phase. Then after the cadets were outfitted, they were formed up in formation to be welcome and meet their instructors. Surprising all their instructors were sergeants, noncommissioned officers and not officers, as most if not all, the cadets had vision. This school to develop great officers was indeed strange and odd, but it records speak for itself by producing the world's best and brightest military officers. Sergeant Will introduced his team of instructors and assigned one to every team of ten cadets and one each to the cadet commander and cadet assistant commander. Counting Sergeant Will, there were five cadre assigned to us (the Freshmen of Academy of Roughful Military Institute). They were assigned to shadow their assignments throughout the four years learning process to guide, assist, mentor, and ease their burden somewhat. Though Alexander and the other cadets were most of the time treated as adults, all cadets knew that they were just children and still needed the present and guidance of a father or mother figure.

The last order of business was taken care of at about nine o'clock the first night at the institution and that was to be assigning cadets into three squads of ten including three squad leaders, one squad leader and nine other cadets. First cadet will command, first squad, Second cadet will command, second squad, and Third cadet will command, third squad. The other two cadets will be assigned as cadet commander and cadet assistant commander. Sergeant Will observations of the cadets in transit weighed on the cadets assignment to positions of increase responsibility. This first leadership team will be the hallmark of the future success of the future leaders. Leaders have an ingrain responsibility and duty to train others to take their place. Sergeant Will gave Wilson the first squad, George the second squad, and Larry the third squad. The other higher leadership would go to Alexander and Stone. Stone would be designated as the assistant commander and Alexander was assigned as cadet commander. From now on orders will be given to the cadets to carry them out in the manner that they saw fit with initial help from their assigned sergeants. Sergeant Will will be assigned to assist the cadet commander Alexander. After assignments, Alexander quickly had a command and staff meeting and the assistants squad leaders went through the process of bedding down the other cadets by assigning them bunks and telling them to get a good night sleep because they did not know what tomorrow might bring. The command and staff talk about procedures and rules and used the time to get to know one another, to ease command and control, in future endeavors. They stay up into midnight and Alexander informed his staff to get some well-earned rest and be ready for the demands, trials, and challenges of the coming days. The next morning, the leaders were ready for training and school; they were up before day light, which surprised the cadre who came in seeing an unusual sight, cadets ready for training and schooling. Alexander and his staff had meeting every night to discuss day's achievements and tomorrow's challenges, but most importance the developing of leaders to take their places and continue a successful command. The important information discussed in the meeting was immediately disseminated after the meeting to the other cadets. The cadets were well informed of today's achievements and how to do better tomorrow and they were, inform of tomorrow schedule. It was also posted on a board in the center of the camp. The new command at Academy of Roughful Military Institute will always be ahead of their assigned sergeants and will earn their respect. The new company will be called amongst the cadets," Alexander's Rough and Ready Marauders" and later, they will be called Alexander's Marauders and it did not matter who was in command; they were called Alexander's Marauders.

The transitions of making boys into adults to a soldier were going well and without undue stress and loss of command and control. Command and control was one element of a successful group or fighting force, which could not be neglected or belittled it was what made a unit victorious or a loser in war. Colonel John's manuscripts emphasized its importance continually and almost to a point of madness. The daily training, of the day, was not routine and the leadership along with the other cadets were challenged every day, but because of the nightly command and staff meeting and the unity of Alexander's Marauders' leaders and other cadets' effort and will to excel to counteract disruption and malaise. Every day went well. Leadership would be changed often given everyone an opportunity to lead. In addition, with the inter-leadership development program, leadership changes did not disrupt Alexander's Marauders, but only made them stronger as a unified unit and team. Each member was learning from other leadership styles and manners, which brought a diverse out of the box leadership approach and style, unmatched of past and present units. Alexander's Marauders were known on the compound for their progress and achievements. They will be tested and hopefully their unity and pride will prove victorious.

The two miles run, extreme physical fitness program, academy study requirement, and the five to ten mile force road marches were preparing the cadets for the yearly cadets competition which all cadet's company participated no matter age, experience, or cadets' combined ability. They would be given the same demanding, rough competition what sophomores' company, juniors' company, and seniors' company are required to complete, and the freshman's company will not receive any quarters or advantages. It was written in the strict rule of the Academy of Roughful

Military Institute. Alexander's Marauders had made a plan to counteract the others advantages by secretly, increasing their basic requirement to double and sometime tripling—they performed four miles runs, increased the extreme physical fitness program, more night work on academy studies, and ten to twenty miles forced marches and more drilling or marching, all the cadets agreed on the insane increases. The vote to do this had to be a hundred percent to pass. It passed with ease, which contributed, to the quality of the cadets assigned to Alexander's Marauders—a dream team of winners. Alexander's Marauders' Motto was "We will always expect more from an Alexander's' Marauder and never tolerate less." The motion was carried, and the Freshman of Academy of Roughful Military Institute secretly increased their study and physical workout to an almost unbearable pace and measure along with their marching drills. They would be ready to compete when the time comes. The companies' sergeants noticed that their cadets were always tired and exhausted, but they could not put a finger on the reason, except Sergeant Will. He knew and he kept their program a secret. It was getting close to the military institute's end game of the year with examination over and finals ended. It was time for the event of the year, which was always won by the Academy's senior class. Though Alexander's Marauders had increased their chances on winning, the senior class were bigger, wiser, and older and to an extent smarter and better prepared to win all the events.

ALEXANDER

Alexander had been talking to the company about all the senior's attributes and they were impressive, but he told them that the better man does not always win—the man who commands a better spirit along with motivation and drive can counteract most strong attributes. Alexander's Marauders must stay focus on the goal and let effort, intelligent, and preparation rule the day. Alexander told the company of the power of unity and initiated the ancient oath of comradeship-an oath of brotherly unity, loyalty, trust, and devotion to one another that can only be broken by punishment of death or worse. Each boy swore brotherhood and loyalty to each other from death and beyond. The pact was made. The company was ready for battle. Alexander will later find out how importance this simple ceremony and oath carried in the defense of the world when every leader at all level must have trust and faith in their commander under life and death circumstances. The fellowship will endure and will be as strong as a diamond in the rough or granite, and worthy of its dying commitment. Again, Alexander's ability to gain the right friends and their loyalty is indeed a character of a special leader. Let the games begin.

The morning of the academy's competition started at eight o'clock. The first trial of four trials was a scholar academy test, which would last four grueling hours. The test covered test questions on languages, West Civilization, World History, World Government, World Geography, World Economics, Government, Economics, Psychology, Sociology, Science, Mathematics, and the Art of War. After the trial number 1, and the tests were scored. Alexander's Marauders were in fourth place with a score of 93, and sophomore were in third place with a score of 94. Juniors were in second place with a score of 95, and the seniors were in first place with a score of 97. The dean of studies commended the freshman class because in the past the highest score, the freshman class has ever received in 253 trials were a score of 56. This fact was good, but the freshman class was competing to win, not just score high.

The next trial will test the companies' ability to march. Alexander's Marauders would be graded last. First, the senior class was tested on their drill and ceremonies ability. They were almost flawless and only made one error; they look as if drill and ceremonies were made for them. Alexander knew that the freshman needed this win to stay motivated and figured if they lost it will break their spirit. The junior class was next and they look good until one of the boys loss his step and turned the wrong way. The crowd watching the trials was stung. And the sophomore class was looking good and only had one more movement to do and they would have a perfect trial and the unthinkable happen. The cadence caller gave the wrong command, the unit could not perform the command without being totally disorganize, and so the company just stop (halted). It was so embarrassing. It was time for the freshman class to drill. Alexander asked the chosen cadence caller to let him drill the company and he immediately agreed. Alexander, everyone knew that he was the best in the company and with so unforeseen events; the freshman could win this trial. Alexander came out calling a serial of cadence that dumb found the graders; they could not believe a freshman could call and sing cadence so well and the freshman company could be so good. At the end, the freshman class was flawless. The end results were the sophomore took last place, the juniors took third place, the senior took second place, and the freshman took first place. It was an upset for the seniors who classes for over 253 trials had always taken first place in all the events. The freshman will not have long to celebrate their victory.

The next trial was the land navigation course, which was a five miles company movement to two objectives in a forest environment. This was difficult for two reasons: the size of the element and the terrain. Alexander had added another reason, command and control. Alexander organized the company into three groups to easy command and control. The other class used a company tactical formation. Again, Alexander and his staff picked the most expedited route high ground, paths, roads, and valleys. The other group organized their route tactically, took the shortest route, a straight azimuth, and used legs. They will find out that their route selection would have been well chosen if this was a tactical mission, but it was just a company-size land navigation course. Alexander's company movement went smooth without difficulty, but the others were faced with difficult terrain and command and control problems. The Alexander Marauders (freshman class) came in first, after several hours, the senior class came in second, then the junior class and last class was the sophomores. The favor senior class was a little stressed because now they had first and two second places and the freshman had a two first and one last place. The freshman class can win the competition with another first place. The senior did not worry about the sophomore class or the junior class. Their competition to win will be a struggle with the freshman class, a class known throughout the campus as strange and abnormally good at almost everything.

The last competition will be graded by averaging the company's physical fitness test results. The seniors were confident that they would win this event because they have had more time than the Alexander's Marauders to get in great physical fitness shape and they have score the highest Academy of Roughful Military Institute's physical fitness score so far. Outside committees of Master Fitness Trainers will test all the companies at the same time in different locations. Their committees are the best in the world for developing fit people and testing fitness. The test will include three events and in this order: The push-up, time for how many correct ones a person can do in two minutes, then the sit-up, time for how many correct ones a person can do in two minutes and last the two miles run, time how fast a person can run it. It will be one scale that will be used to score each event and the unit with the highest score wins with a first place rating, next highest score gets second place rating, third highest score gets third place rating, and the lowest score gets last place or fourth place rating. Alexander's Marauder will obtain a Military school record and retain first place. Seniors will come in second place, junior will take third place, and the sophomores will come in fourth place or last.

When the cadre of the Academy of Roughful Military Institute tallied up the score: the sophomores will come in fourth place, juniors will come in third place, seniors will come in second place, and the freshman (Alexander's Marauders) will come in first place. The Alexander's Marauders will be honored by being awarded the red beret and every member of the freshman class will be forever distinguished by this honor—an honor normal given to the senior class until now. Also, in case of war, each cadet in the Alexander's Marauder would be given a combat company to command which carried the rank of captain. As usual, no special ceremony will be given in recognitions for the classes of cadet's efforts and achievements. The cadets will have a week off and then studies will begin again.

    The week break is over; the freshmen are now sophomores and there are only three classes at the Academy of Roughful Military Institute because the old seniors are gone and there are no new cadets coming to the school. Alexander's Marauders are the last group of new cadets. The school is closing down after they leave. The World Congress has outlawed war so why does the world needs well-trained military leaders. The sophomore has earned a harsh training program because of their performance at the school's end game. Sergeant Will has encouraged the school's administrator to create a strong and more demanding study program and they accepted his proposal. Everyone even the new seniors and juniors will feel the sting of Sergeant Will's new lesson plan or plans. The cadets will wake up about the same time and go to bed later with the new changes. Proven leaders will stay in command longer to serves as role models for new leaders to emulate. One months were not deemed long enough for weaker leaders to observe excellent leadership to do the best so now the strong leadership stayed in leadership positions for two months. The new program has shown some major improvement from past program the school is seeing an evolutionary change, which challenges the cadets' leadership. To the uninformed person, the cadets would seem miserable and over tasked, but to the trained person, they would be seen as receiving proper guidance and training. Unknown to the school, they were developing the quality and type of leaders the World would need to battle and fight an unknown enemy of greater intelligent and technology and farther advance than anything humans have ever seen. The World will be ready and hopefully humanity will be saved. The phrase "tomorrow will bring a better day" once used in the military school will no longer apply in the future; the next day will be the same a struggle for survival and only victory will bring a better day and a lasting peace for earth. The training of the three classes will be speed up.

The cadets' day will start at four o'clock with an exhausting four hours of physical exercise program of push-ups, sit-ups, lugers, steam rolls, and several other extreme exercises which will end with a four miles run at a fast pace with a cadre leading the cadets thus ensuring that the pace is grueling. Then two hours of drill and ceremonies, the cadets will drill until lunch and after lunch military training in class and out of class. They will enrich their math: Algebra, geometry, trigonometry, calculus, etc. The math will be very importance in the use of explosive and computing artillery adjustment. The math will be helpful in other major endeavor. Leaders need to be able to accurately calculate food for large numbers of people and especially when many rations are needed and dividing fairly accordance to proper and accurate computation and that will also apply to ammunition, grenades, and other materials of upmost important. Things as small as living space, leaders need to divide evenly. They will have every day, one hour of survival swimming carrying five to ten pounds one thousand meters, an hour on the confidence course and one hour on the obstacle course. In addition, the cadets will participate in several hour of different martial arts training with world elite martial arts trainers. Alexander will receive several black belts in the deadest martial arts of the world. Alexander during his training in martial art remembers vividly the fight with Neal which could have easily taken his life if Neal had remained focused on the goal. Three hours a day weapon training. Learning to maintain and fire accurately diverse weapons systems. A well-trained soldier should be able to pick up any weapon on the battlefield of war and feel confidence in his ability to use the weapon. Even the weapons used at the examination, the cadets trained on and became expert on at least one of them. Alexander was able to become expert on the entire weapon systems used at the school. Alexander as several other cadets became expert on the use of mortar, artillery, rocket launchers, machine guns, rifles and pistols. Each cadet will fire thousands of rounds each day using rifles and pistols of a vast assortment. Alexander and others will also read several classical books per day to retain normalcy on life after the school. In four years, the school will attempt to furnish the cadets with enough knowledge and skill in warfare that they would be able to command a field army at the completion of this school. The instructions at this campus or installation will be unmatched anywhere in the world. Alexander and most of the cadets, which came with him, are now twelve years old. Their second year at the school is almost finished and the cadets are hoping to win the year end game. Again, the cadets in Alexander's group had chosen him to lead them to victory.

This year end game will be different because of being only three classes; the end game will be a field problem with all three elements fighting each other. When a class loss two third of their forces, the class will be removed from the field problem and will be placed accordance to their performance. The first class eliminated will be in third place and the second class will hold second place and the winner will be the last and remaining class will be the first place winner. The first place winner will be authorized to wear the Green Beret a symbol of excellent forever and command a battalion if they were still fighting wars which the commander carried the rank of Lieutenant Colonel. Alexander's Marauders has already won the rights of the red beret wearer to command a company if they were at war. Battalion would be a well earn position for a cadet in time of war and commanding a battalion will be in a better position to quickly end a war which were the main purpose of the school selecting and training an elite group of leaders. Alexander knew what he needed to complete his destiny and goal to emulate Colonel John, his father and make his mother more proud of him and for him to make his own military legacy.

The end game started the next day. Alexander was cadet commander of Alexander's Marauders and he had his old command back in place. He had his command and staff meeting to formulate a plan of action, to win the war game. His staff and Alexander came up with first squad, under cadet Wilson will provide security, reconnaissance, scouting and intelligent on the other two companies while the other two squads (second and third squads) will be actively preparing a reverse defensive position with an option to go on the offense if needed. Each squad leader, George for second squad and Larry for third squad will ensure aiming stakes to cover field of fire in the company's section or sector. The sophomore class will also use coordinated fire, signals, flares, final protective fire, and radios to control the stating, stopping, rate, and volume of the sophomore's fire. Alexander will coordinate aerial protection such as A10s, F35s, and F16s, artillery, and mortar fire. Alexander and his staff were to engage the enemy at maximum range to weaken and destroy the enemy before they reach their defensive position and get in the Alexander's Marauders kill zone, which should effectively destroy the enemies' momentum and combat formations. Alexander and his staff had called it right, accordance to the intelligent received from first squad scouts. The senior class and junior class were battling in the low plains. The other two companies (senior and junior classes) decided to battle it out in open warfare and who wins will attack the sophomore defensive position from what they thought was unguarded, the flanks and possible rear. Alexander and his staff brained storm that the victor would maneuver his company to attack their rear or flanks. The sophomore position on the side of a hill, a reverse defense, have made a rear or right or left flank attack almost futile. They had both estimated that the sophomores were not proficient enough in fortification to make a defense position strong enough to repel even one squad. The seniors won the field battle between the juniors with minimum loss only one squad. The seniors marched in open tactical formation with a squad moving to attack with a frontal assault with plans to draw the sophomore class to focus all their attention to the frontal assault while the other squad attacks their left flank in a coordinated attack. As the defenders had envisioned, the seniors' flanking squad would have a difficult time trying a flanking assault on a side of a hill. When the seniors' flanking squad made it to the defensive position of the sophomore, they were so disorganized and tired. However, the senior failed to get information or intelligent on enemy disposition in other words where the sophomores' element were. Getting good and useable intelligent on the reverse slope defense would have been hard if not impossible with the assets, the seniors had and any enemy scouting unit would have been easy seen and destroyed trying to get intelligent information. The frontal attack without both squads of the senior was a weak assault and the seniors' flanking squad took an hour while the battle was taking place with a frontal assault of a well dug in enemy force. The seniors' flanking squad reorganized, attack, and was destroyed in minutes. They had taken too long to organize and continue and when they did assault, the sophomore class was waiting for them. The seniors' flanking squad being faced with a dedicate dug in enemy failed. Alexander's Marauder dug temporary flank and rear defense hole in case the seniors plan would began to be successful. The seniors were receiving fire from the front, from a well dug in defensive position and rear from the security squad of the sophomore. The controller stopped the battle and declared the sophomore victorious and the seniors as being defeated. The juniors came in third place, seniors took second place and the Alexander's Marauders (sophomore) secured first place. After this event, the cadets' classes will be tested on their scholar academy testing.

The sophomores, Alexander's Marauder, went to the academy testing building early so they will be ready, relax, and somewhat settled when called to assemble in front of the testing building. This was done to ease tension, which affected the Alexander's Marauders the first time they took the test examination. The staff felt that this had a negative effect on their performance. So the sophomores were relaxing near the formation site and testing building where they would be tested in an hour. The juniors were still in the barrack and were still cramming for the testing (a mistake that will cost them dearly). And the favored, the seniors were relaxing in their barrack and were trying not to think about the scholar academy testing (probably cost them because a certain amount of stress helps instead of hurting during a physical or mental challenge). They were able to accomplish this, but at what unknown cost. When the whistle was heard, both the seniors and juniors had to hurry to the assemble area because the rule stated that participates had only five minutes to assemble and if they did not make the time, they will be disqualified to take the test. It only took the sophomore cadets, one minute to assemble because they were near the formation area. When the seniors and juniors arrived, they were both stressed and sweaty from rushing to the assembly area. And testing results proved that this might had an effect on the seniors and juniors scoring, they were both favored to best the sophomores and it did not happen.

Sergeant Will explained scoring scale and that the highest score wins first place, the next highest score wins second place, the lowest score received last place. After the testing was over, all three companies waited patiently for the results, they all believed that they had took first place. But in the back of their minds, each cadet knew only one company will take first place. It took the scorers two hours to grade all the tests and to tally up which class would receive first, second, and third place.

Sergeant Will called formation and read of the placements: first place will go to the sophomores with a collective score of 96, second place will go to the seniors with a collective score of 95, and third place will go to the junior with a collective score of 94.5. Though the sophomores, Alexander's Marauders had two first places, there were still two more events and anything could go wrong and cause their defeat. The next event was the physical fitness test.

The seniors were again considered the favored to win this event because they had been at the school longer to get in excellent shape and the juniors should take second if this thinking is accurate or true. The sophomore had trained secretly hard and continuously to offset this truism. Sergeant Will was the only cadre that knew of the sophomores, Alexander's Marauders increase physical fitness program. Which for the Alexander's Marauders carried a plus in military traits, the sophomores have performed well by using initiative to increase their physical fitness performance. Alexander assembled the Marauders and told them this is what they have being waiting for and they have the foe or enemy already defeated because of their hard laboring physical fitness program. He added, "We have seen the enemy, and they are ours." The speech motivated the sophomores and they were ready to perform to win. When the master fitness cadres were flown in from the United States (Fort Bragg, North Carolina) and flown in from somewhere in Europe, Alexander's Marauders were ready.

The seniors, juniors, and sophomores were taken to different locations to be tested. Alexander's company was maxing all the events—the push-ups, the sit-up, and the two miles run. The juniors were maxing everything until they got to the two miles run where they fell short by two cadets who did not max that event. The seniors were standing up to their class standards and max every event. When all the testing of the companies was over, it took the scorers one hour to grade the companies and tally up the ranking. The seniors and the sophomores were tied and the junior took third place. The scores were the seniors and sophomores scored a total of each scoring 3,500 points, and the juniors scored a total of 2,520 points. The juniors definitely were in third place with such a low score. This was the first time in the history of the physical fitness test that two companies had tied. Sergeant Will and his staff came up with a plan because a tie accordance with the rules of the Academy of Roughful Military Institute was not allowed in the end game.

Sergeant Will assembled the companies and informed the seniors and sophomores to pick their best runner for a run off and the winner's company will take first place. Immediately, the seniors picked a cadet named Rabbit, a fitting name for an outstanding runner. Cadet, Rabbit, was a well-known distance runner and had participated in mini marathon since the age of eight and he was fourteen years old. Sophomores picked Cadet Alexander who was their best runner, but was only twelve years old (little did anyone know that he started running long distance at the age of seven years old). Alexander did not mention this as not to give his Marauders' false hopes because Rabbit was a national known distance runner. The cadre committee designed a challenging run, which would give each cadet an equal chance on winning. The event would be a four miles run with the runners having a thirty pound rucksack and an antique M1 carbine and the route will be littered with rolling hills and straight a ways. The requirement for this event would be difficult for an adult who was in excellent physical condition. Sergeant Will announced that the race would start in five minutes. Cadet Rabbit and cadet Alexander lined up for the running competition while the companies lined the sideline shouting encouragement to their runner or who they wanted to win. The seniors and juniors shouted for cadet Rabbit and the sophomores' shouted for cadet Alexander.

ALEXANDER

The runners were ready and Sergeant Will fired the gun, "Bang" in the air, which started the race. Cadet Rabbit started in a full run while Alexander started with a fast, but steady pace. Immediately, cadet Rabbit had a hundred-meter lead on cadet Alexander and cadet Alexander continued his fast but steady pace. From the position, the sophomore observed the race the hundred meters between Alexander and Rabbit seem like four hundred meters and lengthening, but actually, Alexander planned on trailing Rabbit that distance. The seniors and juniors had already estimated their win and settled down and they did not care to observe the event any longer. However, the sophomores kept a close observing eye on their champion; they hoped and prayed for a miracle. Cadet Alexander moved up about fifty meter at the beginning of the last mile and during the last mile, Alexander was even with Rabbit. The sophomores saw this and began to get very excited. Then Alexander did something that was unthinkable; he started sprinting when he passed the last mile marker, Rabbit tried to keep up, but Alexander speedy up. Soon, Rabbit did something unthinkable and started walking the last one quarter of a mile to the finish line. Alexander did not slow his pace, but came in two hundred meters ahead of Rabbit. The Alexander's Marauders had three wins and that ended the year end game. The Alexander's Marauders, sophomores, took first place, seniors took second place, and the junior took third or last place. The Alexander's Marauders will again claim the spoils of victory.

The sophomores encased their red berets and proudly donned their green berets, which they could wear forever and each Alexander's Marauders, in case of war will command a battalion size-fighting unit with a field rank of a Lieutenant Colonel. The sophomores will now be juniors next school period. Again, they will get only a week break and will come back to school as juniors. This year only two classes will be trained and taught at the Academy of Roughful Military Institute.

Things was definitely changing each cadet's squad had additional cadre and each cadre wanted to give the best learning experience possible to their charge or cadets' company. Sergeant Will was head of the Battalion training and agreed with his cadre's increased interest to increase all and every portion of the cadets' training. Alexander was at home at this pace of training and it reminded him of his mother's training program, but some cadets were overwhelmed by this mad increase of program and lengthening of other lessons. The first six months were hell for most cadets, but soon the extreme pace and schooling felt normal and routine to all the cadets. The cadets and Alexander knew at four o'clock that they would start a strengthening physical fitness program, which would end several hours after a five miles cool down run and an exhausting obstacle and confidence courses. The physical training was designed to bring each cadet to his very limit of physical endurance and it did just that. Next, the cadets will get a thirty-minute break and prepare for their leadership classes, which will include hours of reading and writing essays on ancient battles and past warriors such as Alexander the Great and Attila the Hun. Then they will reenact tried and true methods of warfare, which have brought victories to several past military geniuses whom feat of military strategies will always remain a work of study and military thought. Alexander was one who was willing to learn and study to ensure his chance to achieve his full military potential—maintaining of the old information and demanding the process of new information and thought which one who chooses will most likely always reap the reward of their sacrifice. Alexander and the other cadets will learn advance management, advance communication skills, and knowledge unmatched by any of the past cadets in the school. They will receive training in advance rappelling, advance map reading, scrub diving, parachuting, sky diving, boating, ship, artillery, weapons, martial art, and numerous more skills needed to be a proficient military leader. They will receive intensive classes in giving speeches and presentations. The cadets and Alexander's day will seem as if it would never end. The world had indeed selected the best and brightest youth of their time because not a one cadet complained, faulted, or left the school. They like Alexander endured the challenges and demands. The future earth leaders will be prepared for what will come in their unforeseen future. When night and darkness came and only then would the cadets and Alexander would get the four hours of remaining time in their time off to clean up, prepare for the next day, and sleep. This pace will continue for one year and without the help of Alexander, some of the cadets would not have last this grueling demanding year. The years' training was designed to bring each cadet to the limit or to his peak of mental and physical endurance and in somewhat it achieved its purpose. Most of the cadets of Alexander's Marauder were thirteen years old now and most of the cadets were looking older than thirteen, and the bodies formed by continue physical training has also changed. All the cadets looked as if they were sixteen and seventeen in a beach surfer body. Alexander himself seems deformed for his age—he looks like a Norseman Viking one of the world first known warrior clan and a warrior with skills of war not easily matched by other warriors. The Vikings like the Spartans were birth and bread to war, to protect their homeland, and to conquer other lands. Alexander could as easy pass for ether a Spartan or a Viking. Alexander's Marauder were preparing and thinking about the end of year end game. The Alexander's company staff had their usual meeting, but this time Alexander brought on the floor a motion to change the company known name to Alexander's Rangers, a distinction worthy of their winning and fighting record. The staff or squad leaders assembled the company for the vote for name change. The name change received a hundred percent vote and the Alexander's Marauders will entered the next end game as the Alexander's Rangers.

  The Alexander's Rangers were ready for any mission the academy would throw at them and they knew that the seniors would definitely like to dethrone Alexander's Rangers and have them eat pie for once. The senior had been working hard to be ready to take this challenge and prove the Rangers are just a second rate military unit and destined to fold under some real pressure. The seniors felt their advantage were that they were older (fourteen) and wiser than their competitors and these advantages would be the edge which will ensure them winning. Yes, most of the Alexander's Rangers were just thirteen now and the rest still twelve, but they will soon be thirteen. Alexander ensured them the spoils always go to the ones who plan well, stick to a simple well thought out plan, and execute it as planned. The mission was a first of its kind, the test, the academy has planned, it was a real mission and dealt with real people who needed to be evacuated from two small islands in the Pacific Ocean. The problem was that the people felt that they do not need to be evacuated and it was a plot of the Congress of the World to siege their island home. The truth was within eighteen hours an earthquake will destroy the islands and everything on the islands. The juniors and seniors were told that they need not argue the facts to the natives of the islands because they will not believe them anyway. You need to move the two villagers from their village homes to their link up points, where boats waited for the villagers' evacuation and cadets will exit by several helicopters close by their boat areas.

A very importance requirement of the mission was to treat the villagers humanely. They would have ten hours to complete their mission given the extraction plenty of time to leave the earthquake kill radial. The cadets had two hours to be ready to fly out to their island for "Island

Operation Rescue." Each class will touch down on their island at five o'clock and their time will start. Alexander informed the Rangers to hydrate (drink as much water, as the body can take without feeling sick) and this order applied to Alexander and his Staff. Alexander's Rangers used some of the precious preparation time in command and staff meeting planning their mission while junior leaders were trusted with preparing for the mission and getting supplies and equipment needed for the completion of the mission. When the meeting was over, Alexander and the other leaders supervised final preparation by first eliminating the food and extra clothing load. Water, insect repelling, light clothing, jungle boots, gloves, machetes, several large flashlights and several compasses, and certain medical supplies will be a priority load for each cadet. The Alexander's Rangers will be unusually light-outfitted for the mission. The seniors took everything that they thought would make the islanders and themselves comfortable; they carried extremely heavy loads in their rucksacks. While the Alexander's Rangers were, carrying extremely light butt packs and several two quart canteens strapped around their waists. Alexander suggested to the seniors' leadership, to lighten their loads, but they would not listen and ignored all his suggestions or recommendations.

Five minutes count down began, the cadets started loading on their choppers (helicopters) and in less than five minutes, the choppers were on their way to the island-landing zones. It took two hours to arrive at their island and Alexander and his cadet command left one squad at the command center to prepare for the villagers boarding the boats and to act as a reserve element or safety net if the other two squads could not contain the villagers. The seniors took their whole company on the trip to the village. The juniors did not have trouble moving in the jungle. They used the villagers' paths and a line formation for quick travel and because they travel light, they could move quite fast. Moreover, during the movement, they drunk as much water as needed and even more lighten their load. The seniors move slowly because of the load they were carrying and the size of their element and the formation in which they traveled. They did not use the paths because they believe that it would be better to surprise the villagers than to warn them of their arrival so they used three separate line formations, which was hard to control movement in a jungle environment. In addition, they had to stop to drink water and rest many times because of the extreme load they carried. Alexander's group could continue to travel and drink water while they moved and did not have to rest as often as their counterparts did. Alexander's company reached the village and immediate surround it and corralled the villagers in the center of the village. The Rangers' search teams made sure no one was left in the huts or surrounding jungle as planned. The Rangers tied the people together in a line and separated the men by putting children or women between them so they could not start or cause any trouble. The two village leaders were up front with Alexander and his assistant commander, Stone. The Rangers did not waist time in the village, but after the villagers drunk as much water as possible, started moving toward the coast and boats using the same paths, they used coming to the village. They stopped several time to give the villagers a rest, drink water, and to relieve themselves. The Rangers did not bring any food because they were sure that the mission did not demand the use of so much energy that food was necessary to resupply energy loss. In addition, villagers were used to long journeys in the jungle without the intake of food. The villagers did not ask for food and were quite satisfied. They were upset about leaving their village and homes. However, their counterpart, the seniors, stopped also to eat, too, which consumed a lot of their limit amount of time. The Rangers had completed their mission and help load the refugees on the watercrafts (boat) and sent them off to safety. Their mission was completed. However, there was a problem and the school informs the juniors that the seniors had not arrived at their extraction point, and time was running out. The earthquake would hit in six hours, and the only rescue help was eight hours out.

Alexander immediately call a company meeting and informed the whole company of the senior's desperate situation and the only help available was the Alexander's Rangers and added that he will not accept the mission unless all Rangers agree and understand the danger. It was a

100 percent vote, yes. The Rangers were flown to the seniors' island disembarking and extraction point and immediately set up and one squad was to prepare area for villagers' boarding the boats and another squad was to prepare water stations and first aid areas for needy seniors or villagers. The plan was only one squad will travel to make contact and safely bring the villagers and the seniors out of the jungle. The squad would be the first squad who prepared the evacuation site for the Rangers' villagers, because they were hydrate and fresh. Alexander would lead the rescue mission because he was the Ranger cadets' commander and a mission of upmost important required him to be the rescue leader. Another reason, Alexander was tired, but able to lead the rescue squad, because of his unusual great physical condition. He knew that the other leaders were exhausted and he had studied the map and knew the route the seniors would take. Alexander took off with a fast but even pace and the Rangers were able to keep up and they drunk water while traveling. Finally, they met the lead element of the seniors. The seniors' lead element was dehydrated and extremely tired from carrying such heavy load for several hundred meters in the jungle's harsh terrain. Also, Alexander found out that the company was spread out and without orders or a leader. The seniors had gone in a survival mode and were struggling to control the villagers and their own squads. Alexander's squad

quickly assembled the company and the villagers and hydrated them as much as time would allow. The rescue squad initiated a smooth quick pace to make it to the extraction point before it was too, late. When they reached the extraction area, there were only two hours left before the earthquake and because of planning, the boats were loaded and speedy away to a safe distance away from the earthquake kill area or zone. The juniors and seniors boarded the helicopters and they were safely return to the Academy of Roughful Military Institute. The next test of the end game of the Academy of Roughful Military Institute was the scholar academy testing.

This time the seniors' class also came to the testing area early. They had learned from past mistakes and now the juniors (Alexander's Rangers) and the seniors waited in front of the testing building near the testing assembly site for the announcement to assemble. When Sergeant Will gave the announcement to assemble at the designated testing site in five minutes and being late was automatic disqualification. Both the senior and junior classes were to assemble in last than one minute because of their location. Sergeant Will informed the cadets to get inside the building, report to their assigned classrooms, and do their best. The Alexander's Rangers were relax and excite to do their best and the seniors looked great, too. Therefore, it looks as if this event would go with the group that was better prepared or the most blessed. The examination last two hours and it was a grueling two hours of nonstop testing and testing did not stop for water, breaks, or bodily functions. After the testing was over, the seniors and juniors waited for the most important result. After two hours of grading the tests and tallying the score, Sergeant Will came out of the testing building and called formation. Sergeant Will congratulated each company on their performance and then read the results; the juniors (Alexander's Rangers took first place with an impressive score of 99.5 and the senior class took second place with an impressive score of 99. Sergeant Will informed both companies that they have best the scholar academy scores of over 254 previous cadets in the Academy of Roughful Military Institute's end games. The next event would be the physical fitness test and both groups had worked hard to take a first place. Again, master fitness expert from the United

States arrived by helicopter to the remote arena of the Academy of Roughful Military Institute located somewhere in Europe to test the cadets. Alexander's Rangers were stretching when their master fitness testers took them to a separate testing area to be tested. They also warmed up by running en route. The seniors casually walked to their area to be tested. The test began with the push-ups in two minutes all you can do and then the sit-ups in two minutes all you can do and then the two miles run in the fastest time you can run. It took the master fitness experts one hour to grade and tally up the scores. Sergeant Will called the companies to formation and he congratulated the companies on their superior performance. He stated that the Juniors, Alexander's Rangers, took first place with an impressive overall score of 3,500 and the seniors came in second place with an impressive score of 3, 450. There was no doubt who came in first or second in this end game's competition.

The Alexander's Rangers had again proven their superior knowledge and skills in planning and executing a successful campaign and mission. Each member of the junior class will be awarded the highest civic action award the distinctive "Comradeship Medal" for bravery and actions which resulted in a successful rescue mission during a civic campaign at risk of life or grievous body harm, thus has brought great credit to the Congress of the World, the Academy of Roughful Military Institute, and the Alexander's Rangers. Each cadet was also awarded the highest award the Academy of Roughful Military Institute could give the honorary, "Warrior Pin," an award that had never been earned and it was thought that no one or unit would ever win or earn the award. The qualification to win or earn this famous and legendary award follows: a person or unit must knowingly agree to take on a mission so dangerous and impossible of success, so unlikely; it would be deem ok, to refuse the mission and the chances of the one person or unit to survive such mission is one billion to one and the failure of said mission will surely result in a one hundred percent death ratio with no chance of possible survival or rescue. Each cadet will also in case of war would be in command of a Brigade sizes combat unit which carried the rank of Colonel and sometimes General. The pin will be worn proudly on the center of the Green Beret's velvet and squarely position over the left eye. The seniors also praised the juniors' honor and dedication of saving their lives, but most important honoring one of the school's motto, not to lead a brother behind. The cadets will get one week off for end of the school year and prepare for their last year and the last end game of the Academy of Roughful Military Institute (the best military school in the world).

The cadets of the Alexander's Rangers were ready for training after the one-week school break, but this time, things would definitely be different. First, they will be senior and now all the cadets were thirteen years old and most important different they will be the only class at the school. Moreover, they found out that their cadre has increased, but happily and one good thing, Sergeant Will will still be their commandant. The cadets last year should have been easy, but the increase in instructors and each instructor's mission to push the cadets to their limit definite changed that rite or tradition. Moreover, the cadets during the last year wandered what the end game would be like, but they did not have time to ponder on that long because training and school requirements were awesome. The cadets were summoned for a class meeting; this was strange and out of the ordinary.

Alexander had gathered the Alexander's Rangers to introduce a change of their name, from Alexander's Rangers to the, Roughful's Rangers. Alexander explained his reasons for the change. First, he praised the company's cadets for given him such an honor. However, he said that their successes were not the result of one man; it took the combine efforts of all of the company cadets to earn their distinctions. The school, The Academy of Roughful Military Institute, excellent instructors, mottos, rules, and disciple are the real forces behind them earning their present achievements. Again, the company cadets voted and the motion was pass with a hundred percent vote to change their name to the, Roughful's Rangers. It was a fitting honor of the hard work of the school's cadre in training them and to honor the school's long tradition of producing the best and brightest military minds and soldiers in the world. Sergeant Will and the cadre were proud of the honor that the seniors had bestowed on the Academy of Roughful Military Institute and her professional cadre.

At the end of the meeting, they had only thirty minutes to prepare for their first day of their senior class instruction and training.

Physical fitness training remained the same; it was very exhausting and demanding. But what changed were the classes, The Roughful's Rangers had several long hours of character and personality building block classes. They were role-modeling classes, serious play-acting parts such as you have ten soldiers alive, and for eight to survive, two soldiers must die what you will do if you were in command. On the other hand, your team of nine is in a boat and there are only enough food and water, for four—what you will do if you were in command. Four is enough to complete your mission. If you do not act, you cannot complete your mission and even harder, everyone is a capable soldier. The enemy surrounds your team and you can surrender or fight what you will do. Will you have your men fix bayonets and charge into a hell of rifle and machine gun fire? This was the hardest class because there was no wrong answer just choices. These were actions and solutions that Colonel John's manuscripts had answered and the solutions were in the explanation of your actions and decision, not what you decided. Alexander did quite well in this class because of the long hours of studying Colonel John's notes and manuscripts. The other cadets were in the learning process because the cadre would explain to them in detail what course of actions; they could have taken and why. Their traits classes covered bearing, courage, dependability, endurance, enthusiasm, initiative, integrity, judgment, justice, knowledge, loyalty, tact, and unselfishness. Other classes instructed Alexander and the cadets on importance of discipline, values, attitude, motivation, and leadership. Cadets did numerous essays on why self-esteem, safety, belonging, and self-fulfillment were utmost important. Classes covered food, water, and shelter priorities. All the senior level classes were fascinating and full with practical application to problems, which could easy face a leader, or commander in warfare and combat. What unit would a commander sacrifice for the greater good of the overall mission completion?

Weapons and tactical formations and combat drills were still a priority training assignment, but lessons in environment survival, researching the best and most reasonable plan, interpreting intelligent gathered, utilizing all available assets and making decisions based on all available resource and intelligent. Cadre told the cadets that some time you must think out of the box and do some totally insane and strange things to accomplish the mission. There are usually several ways to win your goal or complete a mission. The cadre informed us that you as a leader must consider every options before acting; you owe that to your soldiers. Soldiers will trust those who never just throw their lives away or fellow comrades' lives away carelessly.

Alexander knew that extraordinary thing could happen when one used the experience and advice of others to arrive at a course of actions. Some unusual classes stung the cadets, especially

Alexander, because those classes introduced music, theater, and other fun activities, the cadre said that you must sometime during down time with your unit get them to temporary forget the danger of combat to relieve stress and tension. The gun cannot stay cock always because it will then be unsafe for the shooter. Alexander remembers courses covering appearance, conduct, courtesy, personal hygiene, recreation, quarreling, rumors, mess and quarters, equipment, proficiency training, malingering, stragglers, esprit de corps, and many more.

In the seniors' level, Alexander participated in more night small squad level and company level patrolling. They had classes on escape and evasion, which will be very important knowledge to recall at the end of the year. The cadets and Alexander will get very little rest or sleep than their predecessor. They would go over certain scene of the days training in their sleep and put information in their long-term memory which was a good thing. Words like proficiency, professional, productivity, implication, effective, coordinating, inquiry, awareness; issues, executive, exclusion, conceptual, and many more words will become permanent parts of the cadets' vocabulary. The year was finally ending; again, most of the cadets were fourteen years old and looked a lot older in size and shape, like the snipers with the abnormal firing eye the boys had also changed significantly. It was time for the Academy of Roughful Military Institute end game.

No cadet knew what to expect, cadets knew that they were ready for anything the school could contrive.

    The morning of the game, Alexander, as always woke up hours before the other cadets. The cadets never assembled in the large square and this were the first time that they had assembled in the square so the cadets knew that the end game would be hard and dangerous. Alexander and the cadets have notice that the cadre have been running back and forward to the headquarters' building or the command and control center of the Academy of Roughful Military Institute. Also, Alexander, as the other cadets, was aware that two days have passed from the day or date that the end game had always started on. It was about noon when the emergency horn starting blowing. When the cadets received their first briefing at Academy of Roughful Military Institute, they were told that the emergency horn has never been blown and they or anybody will never hear that horn blown and if they heard it, God helps someone soul or bodies' soul. But the horn was blowing loud, and the cadets as well as the cadre assembled in the square of the military institute. They did not have to wait long and Sergeant Will stepped out of the Headquarter

    Building carrying a brief case, several loose papers, and several maps in his right hand. His face was blank. If you had known old Sergeant Will, this was bad news or a die-hard emergency of cosmic significance. Everyone and even the cadre could sense that Sergeant Will was unnerved and he was dealing with a great deal of stress. Everyone braced himself to hear the news, which caused this unusual alarm and Sergeant Will to look like he has seen a ghost. Sergeant Will stopped in the center of the raised platform and informed the cadre and cadets that the Congress of the World had selected the school's Roughful Rangers for a very dangerous and sensitive mission of grave importance. Then he raised a staff of some sort in the air and the ground in front of the cadre and cadets open up. Alexander, cadets, and cadre were shocked. Before marching the group, the cadets underground, Sergeant Will informed the adult, cadre, that they could not follow the cadets in the secret tunnel. Alexander being only a foot behind Sergeant Will, lead the others cadets into the underground bunker or cavern. As the last cadet entered the bunker as easy as it opened, it closed. There in front of the cadets was a large briefing room and Alexander and the other cadets took a seat to be briefed on the upcoming mission. The environment aroused a great deal of excitement and expectations-we must understand these were not ordinary fourteen-year-old military cadets, but Roughful Rangers and such demands just increased their alertness and energy level. They were informed that their end game objective would be a real world crisis, which the school had never been faced with. That the cadets' leadership will need to use the intelligent gathered and come up with a plan that will complete the objective with minimum loss of life and injury of cadets and the others.

Immediately, Alexander, the commander of the operation, assembled his first leadership group, which he secretly called his dream team. They went straight into a command and staff meeting and there Sergeant Will gave the cadets' leaders all the intelligent and information on the mission. The information and intelligent followed fifty highly dangerous prisoners have escaped from a XXXXX rated (an extreme maximum prison center made especially for the worst criminals in the world) security prison and the prisoners had an alumnus of the Academy of Roughful Military Institute with them and another prisoner from a once prestigious military academy. Moreover, one of them named Rock Throne would have been considered an "Honor Graduate" if the school had such an honor. The intelligent rated Rock as an equal to Alexander since Rock was an adult and Alexander was a child. In addition, the other prisoner, Tommy Wilson was a graduate of West Point, which hundreds of years go use to produce some brilliant officers. The plan and execution of the plan had no margin for error with this quality of leadership of foe.

Alexander gave his planning staff one hour to come up with a workable plan that will ensure zero casualties and zero injury if possible while the completion of the mission carried the priority. Rock had separated the group into two elements to reduce control problems because all the convicts wanted to be boss or in-charge. Rock knew that controlling the entire fifty convicts or criminals would be impossible. Alexander's command and staff went to work and after an hour introduce their plan to Alexander for approval and a second detail review. Before the staff meeting finalized their plan, Alexander reminded them that the Congress of the World selected them because they were the best in the world to complete the mission and whatever happens, the Roughful Rangers are the best military unit in the world, bar none. The command and staff went back to work. Moreover, after three grueling hours, the command and staff had a plan equal to their record and past successes. Alexander knew that METT-T (mission, enemy, troops, terrain, and time) can change a well-planned mission at any time. The cadets' company was broken up into assault (room clearing team), support (back up room clearing team), and security (defense team) elements.

Therefore, the last two hours before the mission, at H or Zero hour, the cadets rehearsed every facets or the plan until it was perfect. Roughful Rangers were confident, not over confident. The key to success was to always know whom you were against so there will be no surprises. Alexander gave the go order to what the cadets named, "Operation Round-Up," a fitting name for the operation. Sergeant Will was proud of the plan and their preparation. The command and staff was working on the essential strategies and maneuvers of execution. Junior leaders prepared the other cadets with weapons, equipment, water, and food. Alexander's unit was armed with modified M4s specially made for "MOUT" Operations (military operation urban terrain), hip holster with a 9 mm semiautomatic luger, and several grenades of different uses and purposes. In addition, they wore armor vest and kevlar helmets and they were equipped with bulletproof vests and shields. They were equipped with a Jaguar communication system, the best the world could supply. Alexander will be located with the Headquarter command and control element during the entire operation.Alexander did not like this but it was important that control of maneuver units was coordinated, kept up dated, and function accordance to execution orders. The cadets' unit was divided into three elements: assault (room clearing team), support (reinforcement for room clearing team) and security (defensive team) forces under the control of the three cadet leaders, Wilson, George, and Larry—headquarter element were Alexander and Stone.

ALEXANDER

The whole plan was a plan that Alexander remembered reading in Colonel John's manuscripts and it works without loss of human lives or a waste of equipment or resources.

The plan was simple; Rock and Wilson had separated and used landline and radios for communication. The convicts were armed with an assortment of weapons: 38 revolvers, 12 gage shotguns, 30 mm caliber rifles, and 7 mm sniper rifles. It would be wise to expect every prisoner to be armed and dangerous. Wilson's and twenty-four held up in armory while Rock and twenty-four held up in a school about five city blocks (about six hundred meters) apart. Alexander and his staff and other cadets knew that they had three hours from H hour or zero countdown to end the mission before Rock and Wilson's reinforcements arrive. The cadets are under the command of cadet commander, Alexander. Alexander will initiate, "Operation Round-up," at zero hour by an aerial bombing campaign on both the school and armory. Rock and Wilson will figure out that both installations (armory and the school) are being attacked simultaneously, and they will not make any effort to help each other. They will be in the dark, especially because at zero hour all communications, ground lines, and radios will be seared or destroyed. Several F44s airplanes which gained fame or notandum who pilots and plane gained fame and recognition in World War Three, Four, and Five as the aerial support to call if you are in a tight spot. F44 off loaded their light 40 pound bombs and raped the two structures with the 20 mm tom cat light missiles. This should make both groups go for cover. Note, the F44s have the capability to drop 5000 pounds crater makers and fire 80 mm headache rockets, but there would be nothing left of the armory, school, or bodies. That was not the mission to destroy life, but to capture all if possible without death or injury from them and cadets.

While Rock and Wilson groups are going through a nightmare, our assault, support, and security forces are about to crossing the line of departure upon the crossing this line all F44s ceased bombing and shooting. Upon, Alexander's forces crossing the line of departure; all F44s cease engagement and immediately several batteries of artillery start lobbing twenty-five rounds each of one fifty-five mm smoke canisters (over two hundred smoke bombs) at the armory and the school. At this time, Rock and Wilson groups would be sightless, chocking, and coughing; they have never been under such an intensive barrage of fire in their life, and their control of their fellow convicts will be lost. Alexander's command and staff plans were working as planned. The Roughful Rangers' security forces cordon and secured the area of operation from any outside help or to keep any convicts from leaving the operation area. The security forces were established and in placed. Both the school and armory is engulfed in rubber and smoke, assault forces separate and entered the two main military armory's doors simultaneously with support teams or forces on their rear ready to aid if needed. The large gymnasium of the armory instantly secured. Assault teams start clearing rooms with support teams covering their rear and available for additional support. All five rooms secure and Tommy Wilson forces surrendered without a round fired or without a fight. The prisoners are turned over to a special security force of the maximum prison center. Alexander thinks to himself one down and one to go.

The Alexander's forces quickly reorganizing, consolidated, and focused on the school where Rock's forces are held up before Rock can reorganize and consolidate his comrades. All four elements run in a defensive posture several blocks to an assemble area close to the school. Moreover, with the first phase of "Operation Round-Up," still fresh in their minds the Rangers start maneuvering out of the assemble area to the line of departure. to wait for their commander word to go. Alexander gives the go while elements of the assault, support, and security are leaving the assemble area thus not given Rock if any or very little time to organize a defensive or counterassault or attack. Alexander leaves the safety of his command post to personally supervise. Alexander reflects back on Colonel John's intuition to be where his leadership will do the most good instead of being where it was safe. As Alexander entered the field of operation, he noticed that containment by the security forces was in place and as he entered, the school the assault and support force only had three rooms to clear and twenty convicts were captured and held by members of the support force. Rock and four other convicts were still at-large and this worried Alexander. The last rooms were cleared and no Rock and his men. Alexander looked over the building plans of the school; he knew with the Roughful Rangers' cordon and security element in place no one or group have left the operation area. Rock and his men were still in the school. Stone informed Alexander that they must be in the school heating and air-condition vents. Alexander gave orders to turn the school heating system to maximum output and insert two choking Charlie smoke grenades which is the cadets' name for the smoke grenades into every access port of the heating and air condition systems. The order was carried out immediately and in fifteen minutes at vent-coded number sixteen, two Roughful Rangers' support team members heard cries, "We surrender," from Rock and his men. As Rock and the four others existed the vent, you could tell by their faces and how they obeyed orders from the support team that they were glad to be out of the school's heating and air condition systems. The convicts were given to the special prison guards and the Roughful Rangers were air-lifted back to the Academy of Roughful Military Institute for mission debriefing. The cadets and their commander, Alexander was in a good mood, especially Alexander to service his first real life and death command without a loss of life or injury. He had to look back on the many hours with Mary and his late father's military manuscripts, books, and lessons learned. In less than two hours, the Roughful Rangers had completed their mission capturing fifty of the most lethal criminals in the world without loss of life or injury of the criminals or the friendly forces of the military school. When the choppers (helicopters) arrived at the military school, all the Congress of the World representatives were there to greet the new Globe's heroes, but the cadets just wanted to get the debriefing over and eat and rest. The members of the World's representatives shook each cadet hand and had a picture taking of their appreciation and support. Each Roughful Ranger will be later awarded the World's highest noncombat award given to only fifty adults in two centuries since the beginning of the award in which all fifty awardees received the award posthumously. In addition, the Academy of Roughful Military Institute awarded each cadet member of, "Operation Round-Up," the highest award the school could give, the military school sacred scroll, "Roughful Military Academy," to be worn over the pin on their berets. But to the cadets' the most important award was in case of war or armed conflict, each cadet will be given a command of a Division size combat unit which carried a field rank of Brigadier General (one star general officer) or higher. Alexander, the commander, of "Operation Round-Up" will be given a command of a Corps size combat unit, which carried the field officer rank of Major General (two star general officer). Alexander was only happy and proud that he did not embarrass Colonel John's legacy and that his actions would only make Mary, his mother proud of him and he thought about being home with his family and enjoying family activities and having some good home-cooked meals. But Alexander had to regain his focus because the Academy of Roughful Military Institute's yearly end game was not finish accordance to by-laws of academy end game number sixteen, of paragraph 102, section 5, of page 1007. The by-laws of the regulations covered fifteen pages, and it basically explained that all end games as a minimum will always consist of a company examination and a physical fitness test. The last line also stated that this requirement could not be voided or nullified without a full council assembly of one hundred percent of current Academy of Roughful Military Institute's cadre and commandant reaching a hundred percent vote to modify or eliminate said requirement. Therefore, the heroes (Roughful Rangers) still had testing to finish.

Alexander called the senior class (the Roughful Rangers) to form up and he talked to them plainly. He said to them, "We have just successfully completed a difficult and dangerous task or mission and we have survived and we have come out victorious". However, the most difficult task is yet to unfold, it is can you still complete battles after battles and still maintain the same vigor and active participation it took to win those past battles to win the war. We will now face a foe greater than thousands of Rock Throne and the foe is ourselves in terms of maintaining the self-discipline to continue to give a hundred and ten percent in the absent of an adversary. Can we go hard and strong when there is seemly no prize or reason to push pass or to your very limit. When the going truly get tough, do you have the will power and determination to get and continue to get going. When the requirement dictates nothing less than all or nothing, will we stand united in excellent or with honor and glory or with misery and defeat? Rally Rangers, make your legacy known, and thus go forth. Our goal is to beat ourselves and surpass the physical fitness record we set at 3500 points. Make it happen, Roughful Rangers.

When the master fitness experts arrived to test the Academy of Roughful Military Institute's last senior class or last class, the Roughful Rangers had vigor and a burst of energy never witness in the history of the end games. Alexander's speech had pumped up the hidden forces that are seldom release. They were lead to their physical fitness testing area by the master fitness experts and the experts sensed an abnormal spirit of energy in the cadets. Each cadet maxed each event, the push-ups, the sit-up, and the two miles run. To say it mildly, they blew the test away to another level of comprehension. Sergeant Will and his cadre were without words and confused because they knew and wonder how this can be possible. These young cadets had just two hours ago completed a highly dangerous, sensitive, mentally and physically demanding mission of grievous important and now are blowing away the physical fitness test. It took the master fitness experts two hours to grade and tally up the grades and tally up the total or collective company's score. The master fitness experts had pride themselves on being able to grade and tally the total and collective score of four companies (seniors, juniors, sophomores, and the freshmen classes) in four hours. When they finished, the leader of the master fitness group stood out in front of the company formation instead of Sergeant Will. First, he congratulated the Roughful Rangers on their extraordinary physical fitness, drive, motivation, and will power and they should be proud of their fellow classmates and themselves. In addition, he added that of the twenty years of grading and holstering physical fitness test, he had never witness or had the honor to witness such a performance of pure and continue motivation shown here today. And he and his cadre probably never will again and he said that this is just a one of the kind showing. Silence felled on the area, the leader of the master fitness group explain that they had to use the extended grading scale to compute the grade of the senior's company class, but the scales were not designed for performance of such magnitude. So to complete the grading, they had to estimate the overall score of 5000 plus. The leader of the master fitness experts said that this score set a record, which will not be easily broken or surpassed. The master fitness experts personally shook every Roughful Rangers' cadets' hand and congratulated them. The Roughful Rangers' cadets watched the helicopters carrying the master fitness experts back home lift off and disappear in the sky.

Alexander assembled the company to inform them that they had one more event and the end game will be complete and then they as a unit could think about home, families, and love ones. He then called an old, but in the past a well-used cliché: "All gave some and some gave all" and he asked the cadets which one do you want to be the one who gave some or the one who gave all. Alexander knew the true meaning of this cliché, but the other cadets did not and he needed to motivate his command to excel or to perform to their true potential during the scholar academy testing. All the Roughful Rangers said that they would rather give all and never just some. We have studied hard and long to max this event and if it took remembering, the long days and nights of studying to encourage your motivation that you earned the right to do your best on this end game scholar academy you got the Roughful Rangers' permission. Make it happen, comrades.

The company moved to the front of the testing building and near the assemble area and waited for the loud speaker to utter, Sergeant Will rhetoric, "Cadets, you have five minutes to assemble in the designated assemble area for the end game's scholar academy testing or be disqualified." It took the company the usual one minute to assemble and after fifteen minutes, briefing in formation about the requirements of the tests the cadets moved in the building for testing. The testing took the normal two hours. The cadets were totally mentally and physically exhausted, and they wanted to eat and sleep. Secretly, they care at this moment very little about dreams and if dreams took away from their well-earned sleep or rest, they would say the heck with dreaming tonight. The testers took several hours to total and tally up the grades and the score. They were surprised and happy for the first time in academy's history a hundred percent score from all cadets was achieved and recorded. Again, the unusual happen, instead of Sergeant Will, the Chief or Director of the Scholar Academy Examination Board made the announcement that the company have achieved for the first time in any recorded academy achievement examination's history a hundred percent score for all cadets participating in the testing. The last end game had ended for the Roughful Rangers and they had honored themselves, families, the school and the Congress of the World. In three days, the cadets will be on their way home, they were tired and hungry, and Alexander gave his official last orders to the company. Alexander said, "Company eat, wash up, and rest; today, you have truly earned your keep, dismiss."

And as all the cadets prepared for the march to the train station, they turned to give honor by saluting the Academy of Roughful Military Institute's flag as it was lowered to end a tradition, of turn out the brightest and best military officers in the World, to be encased and only opened in case of an impelling war.

CHAPTER 4

Going Home

Alexander and the other cadets with small packs start their march to the train station. The train will take the cadets to several drop-off points where they will make farther arrangements to arrive home or be picked up by family or friends. Sergeant Will was in-charge of the movement of cadets to the train station. Therefore, he informed Alexander, the cadets' commander, of the movement mission and time of departure, 0800 hours and an 1100 hours estimation of arrival at the train station with a no later than time of 1200 hours to ensure cadets do not miss the transportation. Alexander as always assembled his command and staff for simulations of the orders to the rest of the cadets of the time, place, and order of march to the train station. The cadets were informed to form up at the gate at 0755 hours in marching order: first squad, headquarter, second squad, and third squad with a ten-meter interval between each element. Also, the staff formulated the cadets would only make one stop halfway to the train station for rest, foot maintenance, to relieve themselves, and a water break and the stop will only last thirty minutes. The next stop will be at the train station where cadets will prepare to board the train for, "Operation Homeward Bound." Everything was in order, coordinated, and finalized for execution; the Roughful Rangers were ready for going home. Except, Alexander noticed something unusual and different; two strangers were communicating with Sergeant Will. Alexander had seen Sergeant Will talking to these same two men before twice and until now, he was not concern about their present. The men were both dressed in black suits, one was short, and one was tall and they both wore sunglasses. The sunglasses were out of place because there was no sun or glare during their meeting. The sunglasses had only one reason to hide their identity. Alexander noticed that the taller man did most of the talking and Sergeant Will did most of the listening. However, Alexander thought, it was the academy's business and a cadet should not be concern. Soon Alexander returned his focus on getting his command to the train station and as he turned back toward where Sergeant Will and the two men stood, the men had vanished. Sergeant Will was alone and he was looking at his watch and moving to the gate.

At 0755 hours, the cadets were lined up in marching order at the gate and when 0800 hours arrived, Sergeant Will gave the order to march. It was not a surprise that every cadet was on time because every cadet had a special made watch built for endurance and rough treatment. The time pieces were engraved with the cadet's name and with it each cadet had a life-time certificate to own a watch which was signed by the current president of the World Congress authorizing wear and use of said," time mechanism," this order cannot be modified, voided, or restricted without full approval by a current World Congress in session by a major vote by all congress members. Each cadet was a special breed, a Spartan, of their time and they each had earned this distinction. They left the gates of the Academy of Roughful Military Institute with their heads high and with a step of pride and accomplishment. They had honorably represented the best of the best and the brightest of the brightest; the world had to offer to this prestigious school. A shadow fell on the academy as the last cadet departed the installation, but the legacy of the academy lives as long as a graduate of the school lives and uphold the highest character and personality foster by the school's doctrine. Colonel John would have been proud to witness the greatest product of his military school that he created many years ago. The huge twin gates of the Roughful Military Institute closed.

The cadets maintained slow, but deliberate pace and it was not long before they had reached the half way mark of their march. The cadets beckon to go on and continue the march to the train station. The unit arrived at the train station ahead of schedule and had two hours to wait for the train. Alexander assembled the company one last time to express his admiration, appreciation, and gratitude for their trust and loyalty amongst fellow cadets and their dedication and expertise in completing numerous impossible missions with great results and honor. The cadets here are indeed an awesome collection of the human's ability to create the best and the brightest. And Alexander ended his talk praising the professional cadre of the Academy of Roughful Military Institute for a job well done and before he dismissed the company, he saluted the company of cadets. The cadets used this time to bind one last time as a Roughful Rangers and reflect on their achievements and failures. Then the cadets and Alexander settled down and focused on their families' reunion and the future. Alexander thought about Mary, Martha, and Mattie, especially Mary, his mother. They will be able to watch the sky, the moon, and the stars, enjoy picnics, games, singing and have fun together. He will be able to laugh again a form of an expression that he almost forgotten exists. Moreover, he will be able to help with outside and inside chores and more so because now, he is fourteen going on fifteen. Life will be great. The train arrived exactly at 1200 hours and the cadets loaded on the train, each cadet taking a last look in the direction of their school before boarding. It was not long before the train was on its way with its valuable cargo. The track home was winding, curving, hilly, mountainous, and many straight a ways, but this time, none of the cadets minded the ride. The cadets were at ease with their trip toward home; they talked, and they peacefully slept until their stop came. The cadets' minds were at home and the past was just the past. The train stopped letting off cadets several times before Alexander's stop came. The shades of every car windows of the train were raised to give a suitable going away salute to their cadet commander. When Alexander exist the train, you could hear the clapping of the remaining cadets bidden their cadet commander a happy farewell. As the train pulled off, you could still hear the clapping and excitement honoring their commander and their leader.

ALEXANDER

Alexander stopped to produce a clear thought of reflection and produce in his mind," Farewell for now, we will meet again." Mary, Martha, and Mattie were waiting for Alexander, and when Mary saw Alexander, Mary went into a full gallop, and the force of her charge meeting Alexander almost toppled him, but in anticipation he had braced himself for the impact. Mary gave him a hug that only a mother can give because the hug expressed the longing and loved of a mother missing the present of her little boy. Immediately, Alexander returned the embrace, and she held the embrace seemingly for a lifetime, and when Mary embraced end. Martha and Mattie together showed their love embrace and at the very moment before Alexander was about to faint, they release their death griped on Alexander. Alexander was happy to see and feel his family again. His whole family had come to meet him and take him home what an event and show of undying love and devotion. With all the excitement and activity of the day, Alexander felt into a deep and deserving sleep, which last the several hours trip home. When Alexander awoke, he felt somewhat embarrassed to fall sleep on such a warm and exciting occasion of his homecoming. This reunion and his stay will not last long.

Soon as Alexander arrived home, Mary informed her son of two men dressed in black suits and wearing sunglasses visiting their home and asking her several personal questions about him. Mary said that she told them that in three days, her son will be home and he could answer their questions. Then Alexander also told Mary that he had seen these men several times during his tenure as a cadet talking to the commandant, Sergeant Will, of the Academy of Roughful Military Institute. And he believes that they do not pose a physical threat to them. During Alexander stay at home, he resumed his physical fitness program, academy studies military studies, and war research. Mary and her son felt and knew something was in the arising and Alexander must be prepared for new challenges. Alexander read and studied materials on battalion, brigade, division and corps operatives and Alexander studied battle plans and execution of those plans at those levels. He wanted to know all that he could about maneuvering, fighting, caring, and supplying these units at their varied levels.

He also used time to renew skills and proficiencies in personal skills such as outback survival skills, fighting skills, first aid, swimming, communication, and many more. Mary and her family will be able to enjoy each other for about two weeks until again the two strangers came to the manor concerning Alexander.

Their present was not a surprise and Mary and Alexander welcome them in their home as if they were family or close friends. The taller one said that he was Colonel Smith and his shorter companion was Colonel Jones of the World Congress' special elite force and were here for recruitment purposes. He let Alexander know that they have been observing him since the examination trials and he fits all the initial qualification that they are searching for to join their elite unit. They also informed him that the unit was a fully volunteer organization and they will respect his decision to decline been recruited for their unit, but the country needed him. Alexander looked at Mary, Mary moved her head in a yes motion, and Alexander turned toward the officers. He asked how much time he would have before he must leave home. The Colonel Smith, looking down, said that he had two hours before he must leave for training and intensive evaluations. The Colonel Smith reached inside his black suit jacket and retrieved a small cell phone and said calmly that pick up in two hours ago, and then he slowly put the phone back in his pocket. It took Alexander one hour or sixty minutes to pack and get all the things that he held dear to take on the trip with him. Alexander saying, "Good-by to his family also took one hour or sixty minutes and at the end of the hour." Mary, Martha, Mattie, and Alexander heard a loud bussing. Mary saw it first and she pointed at it. From a distance, it looked like a large bumblebee and Alexander recognized it immediately and informs Mary, Martha, and Mattie that it was an all-purpose helicopter called the bumblebee. The Bumblebee, all-purpose helicopter was designed to be a troop transport and it replaced the Chinook 46 and 47 series helicopters, but the Bumblebee also could be easy converted into a fighter. The Bumblebee had a mean sting. The Bumblebee earned it war record given support in World War Four and Five, being armed with 88 mm dumb dumb rockets and 700 pounds jaguar missiles; it has the capability to destroy an enemy battalion with just one flyover. Its disadvantage is the noise; it gives off letting the enemy know well in advance that it is coming, but because it has the maneuver ability of a big clumsy bumblebee; it is difficult to engage and destroy. There are rumors that Bumble Bee helicopters have the ability to go to a stealth mode and become a silent killer. The huge Bumblebee helicopter landed in Mary's front yard. The helicopter destroyed the front yard fence, Mary's prized flower patch, garden, walkway, bird's bath, and other front yard decorations. Mary was quite flushed, but Colonel Smith assured her that he will sent a crew early in the morning to right all the destruction and she will be receiving a generous money donation for her inconveniencies. Mary's flush face suddenly disappeared. Mary, Martha, and Mattie hugged Alexander once more before he loaded on the huge all-purpose bumblebee transport.

As Alexander ascended in the air inside the helicopter, he heard some noise in the front of the helicopter and as he approached the front he saw some movement. He moved cautiously toward the noise and movement. There in the front of the huge clumsy bumblebee helicopter were his dream team (Wilson, George, Larry and Stone) from the Academy of Roughful Military Institute and the most surprising passenger of all, Sergeant Will (the Military Academy's Commandant).

The group had some welcome traditions to do and then they settled down to talk about why and how they were selected for this most important assignment. After, the group discussed the easy why and how of the assignment; there was one more important item that needed told. Alexander said that each group member, except Sergeant Will, should tell their story of what they were doing when the men in black suits and wearing sunglasses came to actual recruit them. Recruit Wilson told his amazing enlistment story first. He said that you all know that I am from China. While I was out with my favor mule, Jenny, plowing some of "Dad's" field for some tobacco planting, the two men dressed in black suits and wearing sunglasses, with my Ma and Papa, drove up. Old Jenny did not want to stop plowing. It took me about five minutes to settle her down, if you know how a woman can be when they got their mind-set on doing something and she had her mind-set on plowing. Jenny, my favor mule, can be a bitch at time and today; she was definitely acting out. After calming Jenny down, I walked out of the field to see what was going on. First, Papa greeted me and said that these two city slickers want to talk to you, boy. Then Ma and the two men in black suits and wearing sunglasses greeted me with a hello. Ma actually, said, "Hello, Son." Then Pa continued to tell me that they want to take me away to some darning training installation and make a darn killer out of me and who is going to finish plowing the tobacco fields, son. Pa has fought in World War Four and Five. The men in black suits and wearing sunglasses introduced themselves as Colonel Smith and Colonel Jones and told Papa if his son accepts the assignment that they will sent men out to work his entire farm. Papa was quite happy and looked at Ma for her approval. I would not tell Papa and Ma, but I was tired of dirty farming work and I wanted to go. I played as if I was making a hard decision (I had just got home and being gone for four years) for Pa and Ma sake. I said, "Yes, some, and I asked how much time, I had to say, "Good-by and pack." They told me, one hour and after the one hour, this big bug landed in the field next to our family's house. That is my story. Alexander and the others said that they like the story, but for the others to make their story short or shorter. We did not have all year and we should be getting some sleep. We did not know what our volunteering have gotten us into or what hornets' nest we had kicked. Next, recruit George said that he was in a Russia's jail for beating the stuffing out of a wise guy who was not so wise after the beating. Several of the inmates were looking at him as a women and he knew that when night came, he would no long be a man, but their bitch for their sexual pleasures. Therefore, when the men in black suits wearing sunglasses, asked him to join up, he had no other reasonable choice. Therefore, he hurried up and enlisted and within thirty minutes, he was ready to go. The big bugs, Wilson mentioned landed on the top of the Moscow's accommodations that he was residing and he loaded his ass safely on this big ass bug. That is my story. Next, recruit Larry's story followed. Larry said that he was at the Catholic Church and about to say, "Yes," to marry the King of England's only daughter, when the men in Black suits and wearing sunglasses saved his ass. And next was recruit, Stone, he was a drug Lord in Colombia, South America, and was surround by a coalitions of drug enforcement agency from several countries including the United States of America. The men dressed in black suits and wearing sunglasses stopped the raid and enlisted him. This big bug became my salvation. The last recruit was Alexander. Alexander said that he was from an island in the Atlantic Ocean somewhere near the British island. He said that he and his three mothers (Mary, Martha, and Mattie) were still celebrating his homecoming in the front yard of their estate when the men in black suits and wearing sunglasses drove up to their home and enlisted him. And unlike the others, when he climbed in this big noisy bug, he found out that he was put in here with you, butch of World losers; Sergeant Will was not included in this Alexander's comment.

CHAPTER 5

The Island Compound

With the traditional reunion completed, Alexander looked out of the small port hole window of the helicopter to get an idea where they were and probably where they were heading. The only sure information, he gathered was that they were somewhere flying over the Atlantic Ocean. Soon, Alexander laid back and fell asleep and when he woke up, Sergeant Will was up. The Bumblebee Transport slowly descended and landed on a clearing on a sizable island. The landing zone on the island was large enough for all five Bumblebee Transport to land. All the recruits left their helicopters and assembled at a building to the front of the helicopter-landing zone. When all the recruits assembled, Alexander counted thirty-two recruits including himself. Sergeant Will did not fit the recruit profile so Alexander did not know where to place Sergeant Will in the scheme of things. He will later find out that Sergeant Will will play a most important role in their lives. While the recruits were assembling, the huge Bumblebee helicopters left as a unit and departed in a tactical V-formation. The new human inhabitants of the island were seemly all alone on the island until the recruits and Sergeant Will heard the roaring sounds of some type of powerful vehicles closing in on their location. Moreover, as quickly as the noise surface, five Topical Bushmasters Jungle Masters Four Wheelers cleared the edge of the jungle, where they were assembled and waiting. The recruits were only informed to load according to chalk (a military term used to identify individuals during loading a rotor wing-helicopter) and again the lead vehicle held Sergeant Will and Alexander's crew (it was too obvious not to notice that Sergeant Will and the members of the lead Bumblebee had been single out). Alexander mind silently questioned, "Why." Soon everyone will be given the needed answers to ninety percent of their inquiries.

The new arrivers will be taken to an area presently referred to the Safe Haven Secret Compound, but within weeks, the recruits will give the compound a new lively and recognized name-Compound Hell. When the Bushmasters Jungle Masters Four Wheelers arrive at the compound, the recruits assembled in front of a building in the center of five small containers or hut shaped structures. Sergeant Will left the formation area and went in the building with the five drivers of the Bushmaster Hummers and after about fifteen minutes. Sergeant Will came out of what will soon be called Operation Headquarters, with the five drivers marching under cadence of Sergeant Will and he stopped them in front of the assembly of the recruits. They were given halt, left face, and at-ease, and then Sergeant Will began to speak. In addition, he said, "From this day that no one will be called by their birth name. Everyone here will be given a code name and that will be your name and your name will connect you with your special group. To start, you will refer to me as Thunder, he pointed at one of the driver, my second in command as Hurricane, and then to the other drivers and named them, Storm, and Cyclone, and Rain, and Snow. We as an individual or as a whole are Black Operation Operatives or just operatives. You are now Black Operation Operatives or just operatives. We were assembled and created to serve, protect, maintain, and defend the special interests of the President and Congress of the World. We are the only authorized paramilitary unit in the world and any other paramilitary unit would be unauthorized and an enemy of the state or world. The first group of operatives who rode with me here in the helicopter will be called, Sting, Sting 2, Sting 3, Sting4, and Sting 5. With the leader of the first operative having no number just the group operative call designation and in sequence others takes a number 2, 3, 4, and 5. The operatives who came in number two Bumblebee will be called the Lion, number three Bumblebee will be the Tiger, and number four the Jaguar, and number five the Panther. On a bulletin board where each group will reside, you will find your assigned position, a daily schedule, compound rules, duties, and responsibilities. The five buildings, which surround the Operation Headquarters' building are your group's living quarters and the building are numbers accordance to your Bumblebee landing sequence building number one is the operatives, Sting's quarters and building number two is the operatives, lion's quarters and so on. All uniforms and equipment are in your building for each operative. You were selected because of your many valuable skills and talents and the training you will receive here and other places will be only directed to strengthen and challenge your unique attributes." Thunder ordered the operatives to settle in and get a good night sleep because in the morning this ship will sail full speed ahead. At 0400 hours, the intercom speaker echo out operation orders for each group to report to the physical fitness field. As schedule at 0500 hours, the young operatives were engaging the most vigorous physical fitness and mental program; they had ever believed possible. The fitness program was not the basic push-up, sit-up, run, and several types of exercises, but it was a cross between an obstacle course, confidence course, and some mad man's physical fitness masterpiece. Two third of the fitness training area was in a large building about a hundred meters from the main compound area. The other one third was outside the building, we did not see this structure last night because of the jungle darkness (The jungle environment has a characteristic all of itself and the strange darkness is one of them). There were several types of rope bridges, flat, concave, and convex walls, vertical ropes with and without knots to grab hold to assist your climbing, windows of all shapes and types to enter and exit, bunkers, towers, a rope repelling platform, tunnels, holes of all shapes, sizes, and depths, and many more. Outside parts were mud holes, large ponds of water, a swimming pool, a waterfall climb, several types and shapes of balancing beams, inverted and strange obstacles (the world had never seen a physical fitness workout course like this one before, it was mad and madder). After several of Thunder's trained monkeys demonstrated the course, we were told to negotiation all events of the course five easy rotations. Sting was the only operatives able to complete the entire course requirement successfully, but Sting and the rest of the operatives were totally exhausted after their first physical fitness session. Thunder informed us in several weeks; the physical fitness program would be easy to us. The operatives were too tired to imagine that happening—maybe in ten years. Operatives had to negotiate the course five times, even Thunder and his crew, but it was easy for them. They did not even break a sweat and during the thirty minutes clean up time for us to get ready for training, Thunder and his crew had to complete a jungle run in the heat of the jungle to maintain peak physical fitness.

The day would last to midnight, the operatives were trained on stealth movement in all environments, tracking in all environments, scuba diving, sky diving, HALO, Helocasting, Stabo insertion and extractions, boating, ship and submarine insertion and extraction, combat first aid, combat lifesaving, weapon training, hand to hand combating, silent killing with a knife or hands, etc. This intense training will go on for six months and the training became easier as it went. The physical fitness program did not get easier because Thunder would increase the number of rotations when we did not become drenched in sweat after a workout. Sting (Alexander) always excelled in the physical fitness and all the training; he was not human (It was his destiny).

Every weekend, the operatives spent their nights and days planning and executing small unit patrolling—ambushes, raids, and reconnaissance and large and more complex larger unit assaults, defensive, and offense operations. It was close to their first year in training and most of the operatives like Sting (Alexander) were fifteen now. The thirty-two operatives were as brothers now and the naming actually speedy up the bonding process because we got to remember we are still talking about kids. They secretly referred to their "like" as the "Animal Kingdom." The living quarters were the Bee Hive for the Sting's, the lion called their living accommodation the den, Tiger called their quarters the Tiger's cave or den, and the Jaguar called their home their domain, and the Panther called their place the jungle. The operatives' training changed and their leadership changed. Operatives were moved around. Sting (Alexander) was designated as operatives' commander and no one disagreed. Sting 2 (Wilson) became group leader of the lions, and Sting 3 (George) became group leader of the Tiger, and Sting 4 (Larry) became group leader of the Jaguar, and Sting 5 (Stone) became group leader of the Panther. Sting's group, Wilson, George, Larry, and Stone were also Alexander's command and staff. The dream team was formed again and the operatives knew that their dangerous real life mission was coming. They trained as a company more now. The training included airborne operations, assaults, pathfinder techniques, scuba diving with long distance swimming, hand to hand combative focusing on silent killing, reconnaissance, demolitions, weapon training especially night firing, use of night vision equipment, air assault operations, small unit boating, combat medic training, escape and evasion, forward observer adjusting mortar, artillery, and aerial support and fire, reporting and use of all types of communication devises, and mass casualty evacuation. The operatives, which really had it hard, were the command and staff because Sting (Alexander) had them planned many difficult almost impossible missions every night when they should have been resting. Thunder (Sergeant Will) knew of what Sting was during and secretly gave it a go by not stopping Sting or telling him to slow down or that he was pushing them too hard. The operatives had three months before their test and mission to certify their claim of actually being a functional combative special operative group of the President and Congress of the World.

It was 0200 hours in the morning and all the operatives were summoned to meet in the large briefing room of the Headquarter building. As soon as the operatives reported at 0205 hours, Thunder (Sergeant Will) gave the combat operative group their warning order and he informed the Sting (Alexander) and his staff that they had ninety-six hours to plan and execute a rescue and an assault on a well-armed and fortified compound. Sting gave the subordinated leaders a warning order to prepare the groups for a combat force on force and special operation campaign. Sting received the full intelligent and detail of the mission while his staff prepared the briefing room and the battle room for full operation activities. After Sting (Alexander) received the special operation group's mission. He briefed his staff on the mission and gave them two hours to come up with a full operation order and plan to successful complete their mission. Sting informed his staff that two months ago, a known criminal named Johnny Cook, who go by the name, "Mad Dog," and seventy of his cronies (gang members) occupied one of the Atlantic Ocean islands to evade law enforcement. While they were residing on the island, they found one of the ten secret caches (hidden weapon and war equipment supply point) located around the World for a World Emergency. The small group of killers under the command of Mad Dog immediate took total control of the island and its thirty-five inhabitants. The inhabitants are held in a holding area located in the North East corner of the island (one hundred foot cliff side). Mad Dog has fortified the island and he has positioned four two men OP/LP, (observations and listening posts) in the four cardinal (North, South, East, and West) directions and a ten men reaction force. The rebels have been sending out raiding parties to nearby islands to sustain their existence; higher believes their intent is to build enough supplies to stage an attack on one or more coaster villages. Their body counts follow: fifteen islanders dead, forty wounded, and twenty missing, presumed dead. This count includes women and children. Sting concluded that their mission was NLT (no later than) 1500 hours, on the third day of this order in the year of the Lord, on a small island at location, PA54632189, to rescue all hostages and friendly and immediately conduct an offense operation in the form of an assault to kill or destroy all resistance and secure all contents of cache. Sting said that one of the hostage escaped by swimming five miles to another island and he contacted the authority. He will be flown in to make a map of the layout of the island and village and answer any questions we may have on the island, villagers, or gangsters. The staff took papers and maps in the War room to plan the operation; they had two hours to plan two operations, "Island Rescue and Clean Up."

One intelligent information, Sting (Alexander) had to know, was any of the gangster or gangsters had any military experience and to what extent. Sting faced Thunder and with a plain and serious face asked Thunder if any gangster had any military experience and Thunder replied that all the gangsters were draft dodgers. Sting was a little calmer knowing that their over seventy enemies were not familiar with certain mass casualty producing weapon systems and how to deploy or use them effectively. He and his operatives did not have to face another Rock situation. These gangsters were just thugs out of their fish bowl and starting a new business in the island environment. Sting knew that they were dangerous because they had weapon and they had proved that they would use them. They were killers and had already racked up an impressive record. The President wants to rescue the capture islanders and if possible take the murders, raiders, and kidnappers alive for trial. He also made it clear that if the gangsters did not make it, he and the Congress of the World would not lose any sleep over their demise. In about an hour, the staff had a plan of execution. Sting and Thunder reviewed the plan and gave it a go rating. The plan was rehearsed with all concerned and it worked. With all the information, the staff had sold the idea that by conducting a reconnaissance would be taking a chance and would possibly compromise the operation. The mission will be executed without current reconnaissance intelligent. "Operation Island Rescue and Clean Up" was a go in less than twenty-four hours.

First, Bumblebee Helicopter deployed the rescue team (Panther) and reconnaissance and security team (Tiger) teams at 2200 hours. They were dropped out five miles from the island and both teams swam the five miles and occupied their plan positions by 0200 hours. At 0200 hours, team Tiger called and team Panther called; they were in position. At 0300 hours, assault team Sting, Lion, and Jaguar loaded up in their Bumblebee and waited for word from Tiger and Panther that OP/LPs (observation and listen posts) have been taken out. Tiger and Panther eliminated the OP/LPs (observation and listen posts). Panther eliminated the four guards guarding the hostages and moved hostages to "Pick-up Zone Safe" to be extracted by boats (Big Brothers). The boats extracted the hostages from the island. Tiger and Panther reported rescue mission completed. Team assault (Sting, lion, and Jaguar) lift off direction and destination Gangster Island. They landed two hundred meters from gangsters' huts and immediately assaulted using a bounding over watch maneuver. Panther and Tiger will perform security and reserve forces if needed. Maximum fire was used to suppress and keep the rebel heads down and reduce their resistance. It was Jungle dark and the rule of engagement because of poor visibility will permit double tap (double tap, shooting a potential person in the head who might be playing dead or serious injured and waiting for you to pass and he shoots you in the back. This tactic is normally a taboo but not a tactic against any laws of war as long as you double tap during the attack. The assault line was tight and sector of fire was maintained so enemy could not escape and security in place to prevent any enemy from leaving the island. Assault team would fight though objective or target area. Assault reorganized and consolidated on the objective. Team assault lost one operative from assault team, Lion. At first light, mission completion was radioed or reported to Headquarters. Mad Dog did not make it. Thirty killed, twenty-five wounded, and sixteen captured and waiting for pick up. All weapon and war equipment secured and war cache contained. All teams were airlifted back to their island home, "Compound Hell." Mission was considered a success, but no operatives celebrated, they had lost one of their own.

Again, when they returned to the island the President and one member of the Congress of the World shook their hands and said that they did a great job for their World and left. The island was a secret place and the mission was secret. The operatives (Sting, Lion, Tiger, Jaguar, and Panther) had a special send off for their dead team member. The operatives had lost a member in open combat and arranged to bury their brother by giving him a Viking burial and giving him all the honors that a brave warrior should receive when his life ends. It is a fitting and proper farewell to a falling comrade, friend, and warrior. Seven expert bowmen sent flaming arrows to the burial boat and within minutes, the boat was in flames and sinking to the bottom of the Atlantic Ocean. The teams (Sting, Lion, Tiger, Jaguar, and Panther) watched as their comrade burial boat engulfed in flames and slowly sink to the bottom of the sea. Afterward, Sting Alexander talked to Thunder (Sergeant Will) to erect a monument to honor fallen operatives. And he added that this can be done by flying in a huge boulder or rock with a flat surface on one side to inscribe: their names, date of their death, and the operations to the center of the compound. The monument and names of their fallen comrades in arms will be located where everyday operatives will be reminded of the sacrifice and bravery of their fellows operative or operatives. Immediately, Thunder got on the operatives' request with the President and the Congress of the World and within two days, a Bumblebee brought a huge boulder by sling to the compound and landed in the center of the compound near the headquarter building. Phillip Johnson was the first operative name inscribed on the huge boulder, date was deem classified, and the operation was, "Operation Island Rescue and Clean Up." It took several weeks for feeling of the teams to return to normal, but their training did not slow down and with Sting encouraging harder and more training deployments. The teams were quite busy. After coming back from a Panama training operation in the jungle, Thunder (Sergeant Will) assembled the Battalion in formation and informed them that they did not have to call each other by operatives' code names any longer. They could use their real names for now on and they have earned that right and respect. Alexander and the other operatives were glad to have the permission to again to use their names. Also, they will be given two weeks to go home and enjoy their families.

Alexander met Mary, Martha, and Mattie at the train station. Alexander and his family show affection, which were both ritual and expected after such a long separation. Again, Mary made the first contact, hug Alexander, and verbally expressed how she had missed him and then Martha and Mattie could no longer refrain themselves and they showed their longing emotions. It was a home coming worthy of a hero warrior and a son coming home after a long stay away. Mary and Alexander were able to laugh and play together. They went on picnics, dances, tours, and watched the moon and stars, and other things. Alexander would play tricks on Martha and Mattie and they would laugh for hours. It was a wonderful two weeks and it was the first time, he did not have to use all his time studying and exercising. The two weeks went fast and the morning that he had to leave was different from the past. Maybe because he was older, he was fourteen when the men dressed in black suits and wearing sunglasses recruited him. He had been away for three years instead of the planned two years and during those year; there were no correspondence between his family and him. They knew that he was not dead because each month a huge sum of money was sent to his mother and she had men who came to the manor to work on any and everything Mary thought needed repair or doing. Alexander was seventeen and he had a Viking body and was a handsome young man. During a dance with his mother, he met a nice young woman who took a fancy to him and Alexander like her, too. He promised himself next time, he came home; he would spent some quality time with her. His vacation was over and he had to report back to his island paradise, "Compound Hell."

CHAPTER 6

The Battalion

When Alexander and the others returned from their time off or block leave, things had change on the island. The company was to live in tents while the huts that they used to live were being torn down and three large apartments sized buildings and one large headquarter building were being built. The operatives called their new home, "Tent City." The operative training was not affected by the new arrangement; their training remained grueling and demanding. Each building could easily house two hundred occupants. The construction outfit was the wars, the "Elite Construction Company," the best and most elite construction company in the World (before peace) "Elite Construction Company" was an army, navy, marine, airforce, and coast guard engineer division. Their motto was, "We will build anything anywhere fast and better than any construction company in the World. We stake our reputation on that promise. There were thousands of workers coming by ships and helicopters, day and night, to work on the buildings. It took only six months, to finish all four buildings with crews working twenty-four hours and seven days a week and even on holidays. Alexander and the operatives were working twice as hard especially on battalion and company operations. Everyone were being groomed to lead a battalion combat unit and all members were trained accordance to an assignment in a battalion from team leader, squad leader, platoon sergeant, platoon leader, executive officer, company commander, battalion executive officer, and battalion commander. The operatives were training hard. A Elite Construction Company's crew came to the island and built a two large airplane run ways or strips, which C-130s and C-141s could land, and several helicopter pads, big enough for the bug (Bumblebee), and another ECCs crew built two ship docks, which could handle some awesome types of watercrafts, submarines, boats, or small ships. After the airstrip was finished several flights of C-141 came and off loaded old friends from the Academy of Roughful Military Institute from the last four years so everyone knew each other and were friends and brothers. They were to live in the three huge buildings. The Sting, Lion, Tiger, Jaguar, and Panther knew that something really big was going down and it concerned them, too. The next morning after all construction was completed. Several hundred troops came. The last group arrived by several small ships and one Bumblebee helicopter; they were all graduate from the Academy of Roughful Military Institute, too. It was easy for them to bind because of the record and performance of the youth already at the island. Thunder (Sergeant Will) assembled a Battalion formation. He introduced himself as Sergeant Will and he would be addressed as Sergeant Will. They were already familiar with him and his name from the Academy of Roughful Military Institute. Then he assigned a leadership chain of command and Alexander would be their Battalion Commander and Stone will be their Battalion Executive Officer, second-in-command. The new arrivals did not have any objections to any of the leadership assigned to them; they have already heard of their feats of victories. They were already legendary; it was a honor to be led by such men even though in most cases they were older than their leaders. The new battalion was outfitted with everything that the new operatives' battalion would need for training in the morning.

  The leadership knew the routine and had their operatives standing tall at 0400 hours the next morning. Physical fitness was hard and everyone participated from Sergeant Will and his crew on down the change of command, no one was excluded. All daylong the new battalion worked on individual company basic drill especially company assault or attack. Each company worked on boats, ships, and aircrafts of all types. Alexander and Stone studied each company's performance in each combat requirement of war. The debriefing were detail and stress how to improve, not focus on what company did what best and so forth. Each company did live fire assaults, or attacks to fine tune their command and control, to ensure accurate violence of fire in assigned sector of the objective were maintain for two grueling and furious minutes on their objective area. After an assault, every square inches of the objective were inspected to ensure that it had multiple bullet holes in every part of target or objective. In addition, no other standards would be accepted, and the operation would be repeated until standards were met, because these were well-disciplined, motivated, and trained units; all units were required to repeat assaults to see if they could beat the already high standards. Companies' twin M50 caliber security and reconnaissance teams worked long and hard to perfect their skills and the companies' M50 caliber support teams worked on accurate and violence of fire on the targets or objective. Two months of vigorous training, the battalion was ready for any mission or situation that the President and the Congress of the World could throw at them. Alexander discussed evolution to Sergeant Will that the (Special Operation Light Infantry Battalion) Battalion needs to be flexible and do specialized work as a Mechanized Infantry Battalion, Airborne Infantry Battalion, special training in Armor, and special training in Artillery Battery. Thunder said that he understands if the operatives feel that they will just train and no real mission will come. They will get bored and lose the fighting edge and the integrity of this most important endeavor will die or be lost. Alexander, we are waiting for a mission from the President which if lost the faith of our World can be lost forever. Keep pushing your staff, company commanders, and your battalion; the World Congress, your President, and the people of the World are counting on your Battalion. Commander Alexander pushed the staff to draw up battle plans for all types of missions and missions, which will separate all three companies and they would have to fight individual battles. The Battalion has been pushed to their very limit.

At 0200 hours, the Battalion has been alerted; the Battalion stands in formation in battle dressed uniform. Thunder (Sergeant Will) informed the Battalion that in seven-two hours, they would fight a battle, which will determine the survival of World Order. The Battalion Commander, Alexander speaks to the Battalion and tells them, "This is what we have been training for so long and hard, a mission worthy of our blood, sweat, and potential, and we will accept no less than total victory." Alexander turned the companies over to their company commanders. The company commanders gave a warning order to their junior leaders to prepare operatives for war while they form battle plans and execution orders. Alexander gave the company commanders the intelligent before the operation order to formulate a battle plan. Alexander stated that for two years, three disgruntled World Congress Representatives have with the arms of three caches formed a well-armed fifty thousand rebel force to take the World Congress' Capitol and take control of the World Government. At this very moment, the fifty thousand troops have surrounded the World Congress's Capitol and is waiting for their three commanders to initiate the attack and take the Capitol. It is estimated that we have three days to attack the three commanders at their fortified homes at RE56784321, WQ90876534, and TU45679876 and end the insurrection. Alexander's operation order to company commanders and staff, "Special Operation Battalion will conduct simultaneous coordinated assaults on three fortified home fortresses each protected by fifty well trained and armed security force to destroyed security forces, to capture or kill rebel leaders (John Moles, Dixie Cook, and Joe Matter), to eliminate all other armed resistant residents and safeguard all noncombatants such as women, children, civilian workers, and possible hostages and secure remaining of weapon caches, NLT (no later than) 0400 hours tomorrow. Alexander tells his staff that he wants a battle plan in one hour and in two hours; they will start rehearsing. The staff took the orders, maps, intelligent, papers, logistic available and headed to the planning and battle room. Alexander informs his Executive Stone to start planning logistics (supplies) and transportation for the companies based on aerial photograph of these bases or rebels' homes. Executive Stone asked the commanders do they need breaching or special equipment for their individual operation. Alexander replied, "No, accordance to intelligent breaching materials and special equipment will not be needed or required."

Within an hour, the staff has completed a battle plan and briefed Thunder and Alexander of the plan. "Operation Take Down" is a go. Three attack plans are constructed and one plan of the three goes to the company that the plan applies in the form of an operation order. After one full rehearsal, the planned worked perfect. Alexander tells the Battalion if one leader of the Rebel reaches the Army that surrounds the World Congress' Capitol all the effort and sacrifices will be worthless. Executive Officer Stone had coordinated all transportations to three different locations and all supplies and equipment for each operation will be at their staging area. Three C-141 transportation planes landed one after the other picking up their company and headed to their destination. Alexander will be in a special plane tracking progress and available to advise commanders if needed. His plane would be within radio and a few hour flight to any company's combat arena. All companies called in to their commander that they have arrived at their staging areas and they are preparing for follow on mission and they said that they would be ready for deployment in one hour. At 0100 hours, Alpha Company will approach Rebel leader John's compound from three sides—one by boat carrying one team to take out western security post and establish security. The second boat carrying one team will take out Southern security post, establish southern security, and provide a support position with two-twin M50 caliber machine guns to support company's attack. The third boat carrying one team will take out eastern security post, provide eastern security, reconnaissance of the objective, and guide company's assault teams in pre-attack position. The recon team will also give Alpha Company's commander update on enemy situation. The commander and his three assault platoon elements will come by boats through the eastern side and establish link up with eastern security and recon element and be guided in to pre attack position. Alpha company commander calls in that he is in position at 0300 hours and waiting order for coordinated attack. At the same time and almost identical actions, except Bravo company used two Bumblebees to deploy to two landing zones, setup company's base camp or ORP (Objective Rallying Point) and deployed three recon / killer teams. Three teams will be sent out upon establishing ORP.

Two of the teams will take out security posts and the other team will do a reconnaissance of the objective and guide Bravo company in pre-attack position and provide intelligent to company commander on Dixie's defenses. One of the two team whose mission to take out a security post will also establish twin M50 caliber to support Bravo Company's attack. At 0300 hours, Bravo company reported that they are in position. Charlie Company used two boats and one Bumblebee to deploy his forces. Again, Charlie company will used the same execution similar to Alpha and Bravo companies. Charlie company will deploy two boats with teams to knock out security posts in their sector. One team provides security, send out reconnaissance team to recon target, emplace twin M50 calibers to support Charlies' company attack and brief commander on current enemy situation. The other team will eliminate security posts and establishes security position. Recon team guide Charlie Company in pre-attack position. Charlie Company commander calls in at 0300 hours that he is in position. Immediate, Alexander cuts all communication—wire, line, air, electronic, or satellite, and then he gives the go to all companies. All companies attack in such violence of action rebel leaders' forces could not put accurate fire on the companies and within an hour each target areas or objectives are secured by the company operatives.

Each company commanders gave their situation report no friendly casualties or injuries, no equipment losses, and all enemy forces either captured or dead. All weapon caches secured by friendly forces. John, Dixie, and Joe did not make it. Several hostages, civilian workers, women, and children secured. Overall Mission was a success. In minutes the news reached the President, President informed the threat forces of their leaders' demised and that they would get one hundred percent amnesty if they turn over their weapons and go home. The Army surrounding the World Congress' Capitol turned in their weapons and went home. The war of the World Capitol had ended.

After the companies reorganized and consolidated, they were on their way to their island home to be debriefed, eat, and rest to be ready for more training in other environments or terrains and military branches. When the six c-130s' landed and the Battalion assembled in the center to hear the praise from their Battalion Commander Alexander they were surprise that the first person who stepped out of the Commander's Bumblebee was the President of the World Congress. They all cheered and he spoke about thirty minutes on the timing and execution of their most important task. President praise them on their success and said, "With the powers invested in his position, he here by designate this elite special operation paramilitary unit as the Vanguards of the World Congress." He also thanked the unit and then left. The unit watched the bumblebee carrying the President disappear in the clouds. Sergeant Will informed them that they will have three days off and after those three days, he expects them to come back running.

The completely tested and certified operatives will have one more year of training before they are able to go home and enjoy their family, love ones, relatives, and friends company. When their R and R (Rest and Relaxation) were finished, they knew that Sting (Alexander) would insist training be realistic, hard, and extremely difficult. So doing this break, most operatives rest, healed wound, enjoyed entertainment that they seldom had time to enjoy or engage in during training time. The operatives and Alexander knew in their career continuous changes were an unpleasant fact of life; you just live with the punches and stand up with the blows.

CHAPTER 7

Protect the President

The battle to protect the World Congress and the government was over. Battalion Commander Alexander, command and staff, company commanders, and operatives would get a long and deserving break, R&R, or vacation. And after their vacation, they will get back to the grueling training of now being the Vanguard of the World people and democracy. Moreover, Commander Alexander has been talking to Thunder about expanding the training to other combat training such as mechanized infantry, airborne infantry, special boat unit, special operation unit, and many other tools of war. Also, he discussed with Thunder to use the three locations captured from the rebels for training or enlarging the Battalion to a Brigade by adding two more Battalions. Sergeant Will told Commander Alexander that he will discussed his suggestion with the President. After the meeting with Sergeant Will, Alexander went back to his room to shower, shave, and write a letters to Mary, Martha, Mattie, and especially Sally (the fourth and new woman in his life that he met at a dance). When he finished the letters, Alexander was totally exhausted. He thought to himself that maybe tomorrow will bring a better day. Alexander was going to the bed room when he saw Thunder through the window. Thunder was talking to two men dressed in black suits and wearing sunglasses. It seemed like they were arguing, talking back and forth, and eventually, Thunder threw up his hands and walked away. Thunder happens to give Alexander a full view of his face and to Alexander's opinion Thunder looked pissed.

After an hour, Alexander was in his bed and was being carried off to a long and peaceful rest and sleep when Alexander heard Thunder's voice on the unit's intercom ordering Commander Alexander to the main office. Within minutes, Alexander was knocking on the door of the headquarters' main office. Commander Alexander had never been in the main office and figured that what was about to transpire had something to do with what he observed about an hour ago between Thunder and the two men dressed in black suits and wearing sunglasses. It had to be very important to get Thunder to call him at this late hour to the main office. Only Sergeant Will and his cronies were allowed in the main office. After the second knock, Alexander heard the loud and commanding voice of Sergeant Will granting permission for him to enter the office. As Commander Alexander slowly opened the door, Sergeant Will said again in a loud commanding voice, "Come in and close the door behind you." Commander Alexander felt that formal reporting was necessary so after closing the door, he marched up to Sergeant Will's large desk. He centered himself, stopped within two feet of Sergeant Will's desk, came to the position of attention, and gave a sharp snappy salute. He held the salute and said that Commander Alexander reporting as ordered, Sir. Sergeant Will returned the salute and directed Alexander to pull up a chair and take a seat. Thunder started the meeting by telling Alexander about the excellent job, he was doing and in the middle of his praise of Alexander, Thunder stopped speaking. (Alexander knew that an overview of his job performance was not the reason for being summoned, but he was willing to listen patiently until Thunder tell him the real reason for this untimely meeting). Thunder said that you know calling you here and telling you about your job performance this late is bull. I am going to give it to you straight, Commander. I wanted you to train the Battalion a little while longer, but the President sent word that he wants you, now. He is our boss and boss get what he wants. Alexander asked Thunder did he have a choice, and Thunder replied, "No." Alexander, you will be in charge of the President's personal security. The President has been target for assassination, and he wants the best to protect him and someone he can trust will do the best job. Alexander, I will not send you alone; Stone is also going with you. Stone will accompany you on this assignment to assist you and cover your six (back) if you require your back to be secure."

Alexander looked Thunder in the eyes and asked Thunder how much time did Stone and he had to pack, and say their farewell to the battalion, brothers, and friends. Thunder said that he has already made out the orders for Stone and him. Thunder also said that he had already did the paper work for reassignment and had arranged transportation for travel to the World Congress' Capitol. Then Thunder lowered his head and said, "One Hour." Alexander rose from his seat, saluted, and said, "Commander Alexander request permission to be dismissed to inform Stone of his new assignment, pack, and say their farewells to the battalion. Good-bye, Sir."

Thunder saluted and said, "You have my permission to leave, and do your best. I know that the President is safe during your watch."

Immediately, Alexander informed Stone of their new assignment and to start packing because they had one hour before extraction (leaving). At 0200 hours, the Battalion is formed in front of the headquarters' building. Alexander knew that if they left without talking to the Battalion that they would never forgive him and Stone. The battalion knew something was amidst and waited motionless for their legendary Commander to give them the bad news. He praised the Battalion of operatives on the successes of their past and recent campaign. He gave special praises to the battalion's Command and Staff on their hard work of perfecting the mission orders, plans, and executions, which lead to battalion's many successful training and mission successes. Also, he gave recognitions to his Second in Command his executive, Stone and all the operatives who put their lives at risk and endure the hard and grueling training to be truly the Vanguard of Peace and the President's secret weapon. He reminded the Battalion without the blessing of their creator, we would not be able to accomplish our daily tasks and missions. Then he asked Stone to address the Battalion and Stone said that the Battalion must always remember and live by the Battalion's Motto, "If you want to be hard, you must train hard." Alexander named his successor, "the new Vanguard Battalion Commander Wilson will lead you and the Battalion Commander Wilson has always been ready for this job." Alexander turned the Battalion over to their new Battalion Commander Wilson. Stone and Alexander left and went to the Helipad.

Within seconds of reaching Helipad Number One, they heard the loud distinct sound of the approaching clumsy Bumblebee Helicopter. The President had sent his personal, aircraft – —World Bumblebee One – —to transport Stone and Alexander to the World Congress' Capitol. After several hours flight, the rough sound of the Bumblebee landing woke Alexander and Stone. While Alexander and Stone were in flight, they discussed a tentative plan of assuming command of the President's personal security so they were ready for anything when they reach to the capitol and the most important thing they would be in harmony or synchronized. Alexander had briefed Stone on the security operation that he had learned as a child while studying Colonel John, his father's security notes, books, and manuscripts. So when the helicopter landed on the Capitol Green, second-in-command Stone of the World President's personal security was online with the World President Security Head or Chief, Alexander's administration reorganization and purpose. As soon as the helicopter touchdown, Stone and Alexander were out of the huge clumsy bumblebee and half way to the main door of the capitol building. Alexander noticed that none of the Security Heads to the President's personal security met their new Security Head Chief and welcomed him to his new job, which is protocol. The first security personnel who approached Stone and Alexander; Alexander introduced himself and Stone as the new heads of the President's personal security and ordered him to informed all security head that they had a mandatory meeting in one hour in the security briefing room and anyone not showing up should look for another job. Alexander assigned Stone to locate the security briefing room and ensure all security heads attended the security briefing. Alexander requested audience with the President. The security guard at the desk said that the President is too busy to have audience with him, today. Alexander told the security guard if he likes his job, he would do actually, what he told him. Immediately, the President called Alexander to his office to speak with him. There were several security staff and cabinet members with the President. The President told them all to leave that he had to talk to his personal security chief in private. They were stung, but they obeyed the order of the World Congress President.

The President began given Alexander some background information concerning his personal security. The President told Alexander that in private; he could call him, Jim. Jim informed Alexander that he has been negotiating with several rebellious nations or countries which disagree with the independence and democracy of the smaller and weaker confederations of countries which make up two third of the thirty-two surviving nations. The stronger nations want to adsorb these countries. I strongly disagree because these nations are independent democracies and have legitimate constitutions and strong governments. Also, some of the large nations with the nations that they want to forcefully occupy and annex will give them a sizable amount of wealth, power, and control thus destroying the balance of stability of the World Congress' control and influence. I fear in five to ten years; these countries would expect more and more control, wealth, and power and soon; we will be fighting World War Six. Several representatives and certain rich people who will gain from these take over would like me dead for obvious reasons. I have been in office for almost ten years and I have had numerous threats on my life, but it was about policies. These threats are different; they are about wealth, power, and control. My death will would weaken or destroy all the good things my administration has accomplished in those ten years. Potential imperialistic nations will get their way, enslave the weaker nations, rape their countries resources, and destroy their dignity. As long as I am alive and the World Congress President, I will not let this happen. I am waiting for a successor to appear soon so I can retire who can hold the world people together and share resources equally accordance to needs. Your mission is to keep me alive so I can counteract their insurrection and their push for power, wealth, and control. You will know if you fail because I will be dead. Are there any questions if not you are demised?

Stone had all the security heads in the security briefing room. Stone had to tell the President's personal security heads to stand and show the proper respect to their new President Security Chief. Alexander knew that there will be some resentful security heads and Alexander wanted to identify them, especially the one that felt the President Security Chief's job should be his. First, the President chooses to select an inexperience, outsider, and a youth of eighteen to head his personal security and move the old security head to perimeter security, their buddy (John). They could represent weak links in the strong impregnable wall of security that Alexander want to develop around, under, and above the President. Alexander easily recognized the old President's personal security chief, John. Alexander met him at the examination; he was the monitor who paraded his kill for all examinees to see and he positioned himself-center and facing Alexander. He interfered with the meeting by laugh and shouting back where you came from mars when Alexander was trying to introduce several changes to the security operations. John was the first security head fired, which Alexander fired less than thirty minutes in the first President' personal security meeting. The other twenty security heads realized their new Chief was serious about his job and focused on business. Former Head of the President's Personal Security and Former Head of the President's Personal Perimeter Security John was escorted out of the Capitol Building within five minutes of his firing, courtesy of Security Officer Stone. Stone had also remembered the monitor during the examination who took pleasure in his killing of his examinee.

Alexander announced to the other security supervisors that if they stayed and their job performance drop just a little and if he does not see any improvement in their departments or they failed to follow his orders or recommendation timely and completely, they will be looking for another job, hopefully not in security. After the briefing, Alexander had each security head introduce themselves and their responsibilities and duties. Stone was taking notes, which Alexander and he will go over that night. Stone introduced himself second in command of overall President's Personal Security and briefed them on his responsibilities and duties. As the new President's Personal Security Chief, Alexander introduced himself and his duties and responsibilities. Alexander requested that the President's supervisors or heads to stay a few minutes after the briefing to get to know Stone and him and to form a bonding amongst themselves thus form a team spirit and commitment to their jobs. While the meeting was taken place, John desperately tried to contact the President and old friends in the World Congress to nullify Alexander's firing order, but the President would not counter the firing order. The President backed his new Security Chief a hundred and ten percent. John was gone.

That night, Alexander and Stone went over the day's happening and changes in the security procedures. They both knew that twenty security supervisors were too many and definitely will cause a command and control issue with his new changes on how to keep the President safe. The old security procedure half heartily prevent the President (The Prize) from getting killed, but Alexander plan would concentrate on preventing the Prize from getting injured which in term keep him alive in any situation- —one procedure instead of the thirty thousand page volumes of how to protect our President. Alexander ordered all those books to be destroyed and introduced a simple and more sensible protection plan. The plan would be less than a thousand page and easier to execute, comprehend, and read. Alexander and Stone looked at each other because now the challenge would be to reduce the twenty security supervisors to five. Alexander discussed the pros and cons of the decision of letting sixteen security supervisors go and putting them back in the security system after being a security head could cause problem and at this critical time. The problems could be destructive. One issue will the potential assassins look at this change as a better opportunity to kill the President instead of strengthen his security actually weakening it. What will the President think and what pressure will he received because of the firing of sixteen supervisors. The decision came down to what will protect the President. So most of the night, Alexander and Stone went over who will be retained and who will be released. The next morning, Alexander informed the President of the move and the shit storm he will receive. He told Alexander that he would support his personal security chief.

Alexander had Stone to call a meeting of all security supervisors and their secretaries. At 0800 hours (eight o'clock), the security briefing room was full to its limit and they were all seated and talking about their new chief. This time when Alexander entered, everyone stood and offered the proper respect earned by the position. Alexander went straight to the task of reorganizing the overall security structure. First, Alexander explained, that "There will be a mass releasing of security supervisors and assimilation of personnel and that is why department secretaries are invited to the security meeting to make transition go smooth and without problems. Security officer Stone will call out the supervisors who have been chosen to be release and the secretaries will assimilate their personnel into other agencies, which have similar responsibilities and duties. The responsibilities and duties will be broken down in five branches or areas: personal security team, near security team, far or perimeter security team, support security team, and special armed force team. Stone and I will provide personal security for the President and our team of seven and at this very moment five of the President's personal security team have just arrived." Stone will be the head or supervisor of the President's personal security team

The sound of the distinctive Bumblebee echoed among other from the distance, Alexander talked with the President, included the discussion and request of the immediate additional personal security team are arriving at this very moment. Then he praised the service of the security heads who will be soon released and informed them that they will be escorted out of the capitol building after their release as a group. Stone called off the sixteen men who needed to look for another job, preferably not in security and he explain how their department will be simulated in the other departments. In addition, Stone stated that no secretary or other workers will be released and then he ordered the secretaries to leave the briefing and unify the departments. To prevent problems, Stone had the recently fired President's security supervisors immediately escorted from the

World Capitol Building. Alexander went straight to business adding new policies, directives, and rules of conduct and added that all five security supervisors work directly for the President and him. The President did not have any outside meeting or engagement so current security was adequate for the period. The secretaries went back and, by the end of the day, had completed a task, which would have taken a normal fleet of workers a year to accomplish. The secretary supervisor, Molly, who had a fancy for Stone informed him of their completed task. Immediately, Stone informed Alexander that the execution of the security plan is going well. The five personal security team members from Compound Hell were bunked in rooms adjacent to Alexander and Stone. They came in the briefing room and were immediate integrated in the plan, "Operation Keep Our President Safe." Alexander introduced the circle defense plan of safeguarding the President. The four security supervisors were taking notes because they had never heard of such a plan and they like the plan. It revolutionized their thinking about security. Alexander had again used his natural innate gift and picked or selected four gifted, talented, skilled, and professional security supervisors out of twenty possibilities. Alexander's Dream Team had a week to perfect their new security measures.

The five operatives, brothers, and friends who formed the President's Personal Security were the best performer doing special operation training in hostage, security, spying, information gathering, close and far surveillance, skillful experts with small arms pistols and light machine guns, threat identification, and many more attributes. The President's Personal Security Dream Team was the best in the world and reliable, trustful, and dedicated. Every night well into the morning, they discussed situations pertaining to scenarios, which they could face during a threat to the President's safety. On their watch, the President will not even get bit by a mosquito.

The five security departments, all day and several nights, rehearsed attack scenarios of different threats on the President's health, they kept practicing instill each execution of safeguarding the President were perfected. The team were ready for the real thing. The President in a few days of the past shit storm of letting his new

Personal Security chief fire or release members and friends of some very influential people in the World started receiving reports of excellent of this new security chief. Jim like Alexander was gifted in identifying, picking, and bring into their flock talented, gifted, professional, and dedicated people. The actual force that protected the President was made up of about a thousand people and their material, equipment, and war machines.

The personal security force would be right next to the President and the traditional personal security team dressing in black suits and wearing sunglasses would be changed or modified. Alexander changed this norm so the President's personal security team could blend in the crowds of people. Also, Alexander and Stone controlled and had continues contact with the eye in the sky. The eye in the sky being the secret and essential element of the President's personal security plan and its mission known to only a handful of people. They will be armed with pistols, 9mm fully automatic pistols, 25 caliber submachine guns, smoke grenades, fragmentation grenades, knives, and stung guns. The teams have for communication a new technology of an invisible ear attached surgically embedded in the first layer of the skin for incoming calls and another embedded in the upper lip for outgoing calls controlled by the wink of the nose. The near security team was about fifty–to -an hundred operators surrounding the President about twenty-five feet away armed with the same ordinance as the personal security. And the outer perimeter team were the check points, roving patrols, the old lady with her dog, the vendor man trying to sale coffee and donuts, etc., armed with same arms as the personal security team. The perimeter team all under one security supervisor consisted of guards and an offensive element, but most important, it contained the extraction group including all vehicles such as cars, buses, armor limo, air, ground, water, underwater transportation, armor car, armor ambulance, extraction medivac helicopter, extraction airplane, water crafts, and submarine. The last team will be in charge of the Calvary like the Special Police Force of two hundred highly armed men and women armed with weapons which are rated classified. The team will also include several war bumblebees, attack submarine, several fighter planes, and the Vanguard of

Hell Island. This is what Alexander had at his command to protect the President. Alexander instill three codes if the radio communication was being monitored Green said on the air mean the President is in danger, yellow mean the President is still in danger, and Red mean the President is safe. All hospitals within a minimum of five hundred miles radial will be on alert for the President if the security safeguards fail. The codes will change after every event the President attends.

The President had attended several engagements and nothing had happened. The President had finished a speech in Asia and he was leaving the large guest hall where he gave a speech on solidarity and smaller and weaker countries right to exist. He had just stopped to speak to the Prime Minster George when a lone woman with at least a nine-inch knife launched out of the crowd and with one single powerful stroke directed at the President. Alexander caught a glimpse of the knife and parley the knife away from the President and it dug deep into the chest of the man to the right of the President. Immediately, Stone signal on the radio, "Green." Simultaneously, Alexander and the Personal security with raised weapons surrounded the President, the near security opened a hole large enough for the armor limo to drive through the crowds to extract the President. All the other security teams were on alert and the symbolic weapon to protect the President were cocked. The F22s and F16s were in visual sight of people in seconds, the horrible sounds of several Bumblebees were heard, and sirens of all types were going off. The crowds were surround by armed guards facing out and in, several trucks of armed Special Police men became visible, the Vanguard were in flight and ready to parachute into action. Every element of the President's security for the first time in history was working as a coordinated, well trained, and discipline team. All hospitals within a thousand miles radial were calling in to accept the President if injured or killed or needy checkout. Within five minutes, the President surrounded by seven close security guards (President's Personal Security Team) and they immediately put the President in the armor limousine and speeded to the nearby airport where, "World Air Force One" waited patiently. The President was in the air and the word, "Red," was not given until the President was back at the World Congress' Capitol.

The President was safe and impressed how the new bodyguards and security had save his life and had handled the threat to his life.

When everything was back to normal, Alexander had Stone to call an emergency meeting of the security supervisors, intermediate supervisors, and Commander Wilson. Alexander did not start the meeting until after Stone verified full attendance. Alexander said that this threat to the President's was a trial test of his security. The next time, they try to kill the President; it will be a coordinated simultaneous all- out attack at all security levels. We have three days before the President's next meeting to fine tune our efforts, to prevent them from killing or injuring the President, and to destroy the main machine behind this and the next attack. We will protect civilians and noncombatants, but for the combatants, we will not take off our gloves. We will engage the assassins until they are not able to fight any more and then destroy their will to fight. Gentlemen; they have unleashed the "Dogs of War." Stone and I will not be grading or evaluating your briefs, but use them as lesson learned to improve our proficiencies for next time we are faced with this foe. The sectors did not discuss their achievement but failures in their actions and how they can improve them. Alexander said that they let the crowd get too close to the President and next time a rope lane will be instructed and he will tell the President to only shake hands with short sleeves and limit his hand shaking in a hostile environment. He is going to suggest strongly for the President to wear a bullet and knife proof vest. We will also have a bulletproof blanket to throw over the President while waiting for extraction. He added several more items his team discussed and ended the meeting telling all security supervisors, support teams, and special operators that the President is alive and well because of their actions and I am going to speak for the President, "Thanks."

The President is scheduled to visit a summit in the dead zone to negotiate a nonaggression treaty and to renew old friendly ties. The dead zone makes up about one third of the population on the earth after the big war, World War Five. The several million people is ruled by King Sam (who use to be a janitor at some small rural school in the country before the war). He is now their unchallenged

ALEXANDER

ruler and rule the Dead Zone with an iron fist. There are several thousand people in the dead zone, which would love to take credit for the death of the World Congress' President. They had demonstrated for over ten years against the World Congress stopping them from invading two bordering countries and taking over their resources. With Alexander controlling his safety, the President felt confident in his personal security and safety, which for ten years, he would not even contemplated a meeting in the Dead Zone or any other countries that seasonally burn the World Congress' Flag. However, the President is no fool; he knows that there will be an attempt on his life, he feels that his Personal Security is in excellent hand with his new security, Dream Team and for two year, it has proven successful under Alexander's leadership as the President's Personal Security Chief. Alexander is twenty years old now and is engaged to Sally and they have two boys (John and Stone). Mary, Martha, and Mattie love when Alexander and his family visit the old manor on some unknown island in the Atlantic Ocean. Family life have not slowed Alexander down; he is still as sharp as a tack. For six months, Alexander and his security advisors have been planning a detail security plan to safeguard the President. Every things were in place and the next day, the President with other members of the World Congress would be taking Air Force One and landing in the Dead Zone. Alexander and Stone flew with the President while the other personal security guards over watched the Flight in F22s, F35s, and several well-armed Bumblebees. Alexander monitors all security nets and especially the eye in the sky. Each element reported all is well at home. The security force will be on a twenty-four hour every day- —hot status while on this mission. The President, Alexander, and Stone were relaxed, but the other security sector leaders, you probably could not put a needle in their anuses and this is just what Alexander wanted a high alert readiness. The President would be in the Dead Zone for five days starting Monday, which he will visit, King Sam at a formal banquet in which protocol prohibit business being discussed or addressed in any form. The next day, Tuesday, was spent meeting King Sam's large family and again business was tabooed. Tuesday, sectors' reports were Good Night, Honey. The third day, Wednesday, and all reports from the security sector were Ma is sleeping. Thursday would be definitely different. The eye in the sky reported about hundred miles out large troop movement from east to west at a rate of movement estimated time of arrival at their location 1300 hours (one o'clock). Alexander informed Stone and the President. Alexander authorized a secret night mass tactical combat parachute descent by the Vanguard Battalion. The Vanguard Battalion was alerted for a combat parachute dropped to execute a blocking position (defensive position) dig in with a follow on mission to turn offensive. Every thing was going as plan. The assassins were not aware of the Vanguard's defensive position just fifty miles from the huge Summit briefing room. The Summit had gone well and the President had complete the Nonaggression Pact and renewed old friendly ties. At noon, Thursday, the President started his friendship speech and ended it about (1230 hours) 12:30 p.m. and he was leaving the building when the far perimeter security alerted Alexander of heavily armed people in four vans heading to their location from all cardinal (east, west, north, and south) directions estimated time of arrival twenty minutes. Alexander gave them the order to take them out and gave over watch the order to reduce enemy forces heading toward Vanguard Battalion's defense position. Several F22's, several F35's, several F16's, several A10's, AC130's, B52's, Bumblebees, and several other fighters came out of nowhere and surprise the army moving to the Dead Zone Capitol to kill the World President. It was a turkey shoot and when they finished, there were only enough enemy left to improve their weapon proficient score, because Alexander gave the Vanguard orders to go on the offense and rule of engagement open season on the bad guys. After about five minutes, Over Watch reported mission success, Special Police reported all vans destroyed and all rebels dead, and the Vanguard reported work in process. All reported no friendly casualties. The President's life was still in danger. He was walking out along the corridor stringed off as discussed when four armed men burst though the tape off area. Thunder and Stone took out two men with their 9mm clocks, but the other two men were too close to shot so Stone did a right turn fly kick sending his man to the ground and Alexander used a knife slash with the hand catching the man in the throat. Stone gave his man a hammer blow to the back of the head and a neck chock and finished him off by breaking his neck. Alexander finished his second man with a kick to the head, a body drop into the man's chest, and he went slump. Alexander called for immediate evacuation to safety.

Friday security was still in place and the day was event free. When the President reaches the World Congress's Capitol, he said to Alexander that it was time to retire and he has found his replacement.

CHAPTER 8

President Alexander

The next day, the President addressed the World Congress and informed them of the results of the summit in the Dead Zone with the Dictator Jim. After all the business of the World Congress' representatives, he called for a special session. Within thirty-minutes, they came out and called the President's Personal Security Chief, Alexander to report to the World Congress. The President informed Alexander in the present of a full present World Congress of his hundred percent election to take over the President of the World Congress. Alexander said that he must ask his mother and girlfriend if he can accept the job of President of the World Congress. The World Representatives laughed at his reply. The President gave Alexander and Stone a month leave for a job well done. All the President's dangerous meetings were finished and Alexander and Stone's subordinate leaders could secure the President now.

Alexander enjoyed his vacation with his mother and co-mothers, Martha and Mattie. Alexander was also spending a lot of time with Sally (his girlfriend and mother of two boys). Everyone loved Sally; she was a very intelligent, kind, and beautiful women. She was very mature for her age and Alexander loved her. The second week at home, Alexander informed Mary that he had something very importance to tell her. She said that she knows that he wanted to marry Sally. Alexander said that she was right, but that was the second discussion. Alexander told Mary that he has been offered the position of President of the World Congress and he is asking her should and can he accept the position. Mary was stung with joy and had to call her partners in life, Martha and Mattie. Martha and Mattie came running thinking that there was a fire or serious accident. When they reached Mary and Alexander, they were completely exhausted and would not been of any help in the case of a real disaster. Mary caught her breath and excitedly told Martha and Mattie that they were in the present of the next President of the World Congress. Martha and Mattie practically almost fainted. They all hugged him and congratulated him and then there were a two minutes pause and silence. All three Mary, Martha, and Mattie simultaneously asked him have he told Sally. Alexander replied, "No." They were so over joy that acting as they were mad at his reply was so obviously fake. Mary in front of her life long companions said, "Yes, Alexander, you have my permission to be President of the World Congress and my blessing to marry Sally." Martha and Mattie were surprise at that last statement and they were twice as happy if that is possible. They hugged Alexander again and they said that his hard work deserved both good fortunes and happiness. Later that day when Sally and Alexander were at the lake in front of the manor, Alexander asked Sally to marry him and she accepted his proposal before he had finished proposing. He said, "Future First Lady, we'll get married in the Capitol building of the World." Sally laughed and said that she loves him, but sometime, he can be very imaginative. He then told Sally of his appointment. After the month, upon Alexander returned he accepted the office only if his vice president and personal advisor was Stone. Immediate, they granted his wish and he was sworn in the next week with Sally, Mary, Martha, and Mattie at his side and representatives of the people, rulers, leaders, and people of the World present during his inauguration. Millions of the World people watched Alexander sworn in and inauguration on television, listen to it on radios, or monitored it on some other devises. A week later, Alexander and Sally and Stone and Molly were married in the World Capitol's largest guest auditorium. President Alexander made sure that Former President Jim received the recognition and respected that he deserved sending him and his wife to their retirement resort. It was a World celebration of President Jim's legacy and ability to hold the World's nation together after World War Five. As Former President Jim and Former President's First Lady, Sue entered, World Air Force One leaving for their Paradise resort in the sun. President Alexander said, "Farewell Brother."

For the next two years, Alexander had reinforced the Former President's policy of good will to all nations of the World. Mary, Martha, and Mattie had made several visits to the World of Congress' White House. They had their own rooms reserved and they helped take care of the two baby boys that Sally and Alexander had managed to create between their busy schedules. President Alexander was an excellent husband and father. First Lady Sally and President Alexander visited all thirty-two nations. As President Alexander, Alexander been well read in past and present World Affairs, he passed bills after bills to improved Worldism, the love of World unity, improved education opportunities for everyone no matter where you lived, improved ways to take care of the sick, poor, and mentally ill. He had a world pledge created so the children and the adults of the world would love themselves, fellow members of the world and figurative the world itself. Special committees were formed for just about every important issue to reduce the stress or eliminate the problem. The President pushed farming, building infrastructures, factory, building more airports, planes, cars, trucks, installing land lines to all nations, radio communication with all nations, internet communication with all nation, encouraged international brotherhood, sports of all types, yearly fun nations Olympus games, appreciation in multicultural arts, etc. Everything you could imagined; this was a two year period which we could called the "Era of Enlightenment of the World Peoples." Two wonderful years had passed, and the President had kept in touch with the Former President Jim, his friend, and had regular meeting with Sergeant Will and his operative's brothers. All ten caches were uncovered and held on the secret island installation named by its occupants, "Compound Hell." Sally was with child and Alexander and Sally hoped that the baby would be a girl to keep the boys in line. It was late; Alexander and Sally were about to call it a night when a special agent of his special communication division, old friend, and the eye in the sky department head, informed the President of an urgent message which have just been decoded.

President Alexander of the World Congress with several of his top advisors received a secret message through the President top-secret secure electronic messages communication transmitter and receiver from an alien race. The receiver registered also the location where the message originated and the President knew that the message did not come from a prankster hacker who had some way hacked into the top-secret message system main frame. The message was from an alien species light years away from earth. The message was taken extremely serious so the President called an emergency special meeting at 0200 hours (two o'clock or 2:00 a.m.) in the morning to convene at 0400 hours (four o'clock or 4:00 a.m.) in the morning. The message stated that in five years, the aliens would invade the earth and enslave its inhabitants. The message also informed the leaders of earth that they were very much like them, but they are highly intelligent and they have superior weapons and millions of storm troopers. They would like to execute a peaceful enslavement of the planet, earth, but they are prepared to go to war so it will be to the earth people salvation to prepare the earth for a peaceful servitude existence. The message ended with the message that resistance would be futile.

The message was on a big screen on the sidewall for all essential leaders to read before the meeting was call to order. Representatives of each of the thirty-two nations, the President's cabinet, the special advisors, Sergeant Will, and Commander Wilson of the Vanguard Battalion, and representatives of a group only called in time of a crisis (the Black Team) were present. Vice-President Stone called the meeting to order. The President Alexander held the floor and he said that the message shown on the sidewall which they have read is not a hoax. This message was received about two hours ago and we are here to debate what are the free people of the World going to do. As President of the World Congress and Superior Military Commander of the World War Machine, I already know what to do, but in a democracy and specially a decision of this magnitude, I need your dedication, support, assistance, and hold heartily blessing. The voting ballets are being passed out at this moment for a secret vote on one of the two choices, we have to submission or to go to war. President Alexander ended his initiated speech, "Let your conscience be your guide."

After five minutes, voting was finished, and the ballot box was collected. He selected Sergeant Will to come up and read out the results of the voting. All thirty-two votes favored war. The President was proud of the results of the voting and he addressed the group that they will try several attempts to negotiate a peaceful solution to the invaders while the wheel of preparing for war will be up. "My war command and staff need to stay and the rest of you need to alarm the world of this threat. The people of earth are used to war and being truthful to them will only enrage their innate need to maintain their creator's gift of freedom. Is there any question?" Pause. "If there are no questions, this special world meeting is closed."

Once everyone except the ones needed to plan for possible armed conflict have left, Alexander invited the rest in the World of Congress War Room. Stone and helper had to break the seal on the main door of the war room, the President and several advisors had to enter special codes, and the President had to use his voice command and pass word to open the war room. The World Congress' War Room had been breached or open. Alexander had also before the meeting alerted the Past President (Jim) to be involved in this endeavor. Everyone in the War Room was surprise to see the old President again and all stood and showed him the respect of a past President, which he earned. Alexander nod to Jim and began his briefing. This is what we know about this potential enemy, they are an intelligent alien human race and we presumed that they need the basic essential things that we need for survival. Since they are preparing to invade earth, we can assume that those basis items are limited resource to them and they want to confiscate some or most of our resources and enslave us to manufacture and grow supplies for their survival. They are on their way to earth with a large fleet and millions of storm troopers and have air ships and superior weapons. We are at a disadvantage because we have only a limit arsenal of weapons of war.

We chose to fight or war if a peace arrangement cannot be negotiated. I am not going to initiate a War Draft, but enlist the World's able fighter from seven years old to seventy years old. I am going to distribute where needed, the war systems of the ten caches of the World. We are going to not consolidation for this war, but we will fight in the seven continents of the World to disperse their forces or war machine. We are going to use techniques of war developed and used before modern weapon systems and tactics. Leaders familiar with ancient and past weapons of all world regions will be dispatch to prepare them for the war to come in five years. All noncombatants would, if they were able, will be our home front and reasons for our sacrifice and for fighting, our motivation will be our driving force, and reason for our diligent unwavering and unrelenting fighting and efforts. We will make communication system in all forms to talk, assist, resupply, pass intelligent, and more. It will be a long war, but they can be killed, hurt, and demoralized. We will at the right time channel them in a web of kill zones, a final decisive battle will be fought, and the victor will claim its rewards.

President Alexander of the World Congress informed the President's Former President Jim, Sergeant Will, Vice-President Stone, his personal cabinet, Special Operation Head, Communication and technology adviser, Energy and Power adviser, Disease and Biological Adviser, Chemical and Mineral Adviser, Black Operation Adviser, World Affairs Adviser, et al., to lay out a five year plan from today that is attainable and workable. The purpose of the plan must be to combat an unknown invading intelligent human race of aliens with sophisticated weapons, equipment, and material bent on invading, enslaving, taking, and stripping us of our dignity and freedom. They have superiors, weapons, aerial battle ships, aerial command vessels, storm troopers, and hell knows what else. You have five hours to come up with a manageable, reasonable, simple, cost effective, and a plan that I can sell to the World leaders and people. Let us make it happen. Failure is no option.

President Supreme Commander Alexander stayed in the war room during the process of planning to repel the coming alien invasion to answer questions, keep the team focus on the task, his present emphasis the importance of the task, and to ensure his intent is fully understood of how he want to fight the world intruders. And surprising in four hours, the team of planners had finished their Commander's Operation Plan. Sergeant Will was selected to brief the President and World Representatives on the plan and its execution. The first thing, Sergeant Will said that, "Operation Endurance for Alien Expulsion," has many complicated phases the first phase is to alert the leaders and people of the incoming threat and to mobilize a World at all social and society level to get one hundred percent involved in this long term endeavor. Caves, Caverns, tunnels, and underground shelter need to be identified and prepared for long time human occupation and living environments. Masses construction of underground fortress and fortifications need to made where all the World people can be safely hidden and protected if the need arrives. Present large known caves and caverns around the World need to be used for storing and residing places for insurgents, guerrilla, and armies of varies war capabilities (light infantry, airborne infantry, artillery units, armor units, etc.,) and all makes and forms of support elements (medical, food, war supplies, etc.). All aircrafts of all types (F22, F16, F35, Bumblebees Helicopters, C-130's, C-141, C-23's, etc.) need underground bases. The World must be literary grounded. Phase Two, all caches, weapons of all and any type (new, old, or ancient) must be available to the masses especially to armed forces. Modern and old (blacksmith) factories must make the quality and quantity of weapons and ammunitions needed to fight a war of this magnitude. Countries need to develop several ways to communicated kills, losses, and needs. A complicated system of support of basis survival essential need to be shared fairly and trust between countries must be always maintain even during trying and futile times. Phase Three, all advance interspace missiles, intercontinental missiles, subspace missiles, intracontinental missiles, continent missiles, rocket launchers, and all other surface to air missile systems of all grades and capability need to be integrated in the overall security of the World. Disease, Biological, Chemical, and Nuclear hardware need to be integrated in the overall scheme of defensive and offensive weapon collaboration. Phase four, all types of non-decisive military engagement tactics including dirty tricks, terrorist attacks, espionage, shoot and scoot tactics, spider holes, firing from trees, small scale raids, ambushes, attacks, uses of mines in roads, trails, paths, etc., blowing up bridges, their war machines, etc. The ingenuity of the human mind must invent ways, methods, and a system to wear down the invaders. The alien should see no sleep, rest, or safe moment while on earth. Combat twenty-four hours and seven days a week without let up, it should and must be relentless. Phase Five, engage enemy at the maximum effective range of our modern technology and ancient weapon system. Leave no food source on surface earth for them to eat or good clean water (do not poison the water) but you can make it distasteful for the time they are here. If you can introduce drugs, alcohol, and cigarettes, and set off volcanoes, channel the enemy aircraft and ground troops in the worst areas of the world, places we have difficulty surviving. Phase Six, All earth people need to be efficient and proficient in survival skills, using fire to destroy enemy, water to destroy enemy by destroying dams, weather and nature, camouflage, stealth, silence killing, hand to hand, use of killing with knives, land navigation, reporting accurate information, use of weapons, etc. Alexander added something he read in the notes of Colonel John. It pertained to the defense of Spartan because Spartans did not have a wall around it like most small or big city. A Spartan replied that every Spartan was a brick that made their wall. That is the way; I want the World people to feel, Sergeant Will continued with the briefing. Phase Seven: military leaders of all era will be distributed to all corners of the World to prepare and train the world of the coming calamity. It will be a potentially long difficult struggle, but the World will bear the burden of the symbolic storm approaching our planet. Phase Eight: Any and all amateur and advanced radar, tracking systems, and radios will be used to identify, locate, gather intelligent on enemy's people and vessels for destruction or attack. All the phase will be taking place simultaneously and new discovery and improvement will be added to the Phases. Information is already coming in of World people being discovered living hidden from our awareness for almost twenty years living in the underground environment of our world. Reports say they are well armed and have military experience and will become allies when ask or needed. They have been monitoring the progress of the World for years and like the direction it is heading and an attack on the surface and what they call surface people is an attack on them. They have love ones, families, and friends who will be endangered. They also live on the resources of the earth and the alien wants those limited resources, which will threaten their lives, too. And Phase Nine: Supreme Commander Alexander informed the staff planners that the initial negotiation with the alien has fail to bear fruit and he has doubts that the alien will reason sensible on their plea for a peaceful solution. They want domination, power, and total control (enslavement). Phase Nine will be a continue effort or will be efforts to reason a peaceful solution by means of a treaty, co-occupation, trade or commerce solution, immigration solution, nonaggression pact, earth corporation or collaboration solution. If all negotiations fail, war will be forced on the people of the earth. Supreme Commander Alexander was pleased with their plan and informed them to execute it now and that he wants to meet with the leaders of this hidden people. "Operation Endurance for Expulsion," is in effect. After Sergeant Will introduction of the nine phases that the team planned, Sergeant Will took his seat and Alexander stood up and momentarily paused. Supreme Commander Alexander said that if all effort fails; he will initiate or authorizes, "The Doom Day Solution" (Phase ten): The Supreme World Military Commander Alexander will broadcast to the world people if the alien humans prove to be of such beasts, predators, or creatures that he will authorize extreme world offensive order—crack egg shell 000000001. "The Dogs of Hell" will be released with this supreme order to legally without forethought, use extreme prejudice, and malice (maliciously exercised) thus authorizing no quarters with possibility of "Armageddon" consequences leading to "Apocalypse' results.

During the third year, earth's advanced radars picked up the alien's Armanda several hundred lightrons away from earth in space with a trace direction heading straight to the planet earth. The radars were able to clearly make out about a billion space crafts and one huge spaceship in the center of the Armanda or fleet. Alexander was heard saying, "Bless us," and gave the order to execute, "Operation Out Reach." As soon as Alexander gave the order, hundreds of thousands super long range space travel Titan missiles armed with warhead filed with the earth's once most deadliest diseases left their secret unground, mountainous, sea, submarines, and ocean bed pads. The missiles will penetrate the body of their space ships and they will laugh on how weak the earth's planet defensive are, but inside each missile several deadest human diseases such as Small Pox, the Black Death, Blunios Plague and more would have made their destructive home on their ships. The President will give order to launch every missile of death. After a year, again Alexander try to reason with the aliens and they refuse to negotiate. His pleas fell on deaf ears.

And on the fourth year, earth's advanced radars locate the Alien's Armanda, but now, it hundreds of millions short of the might one billion a year ago. Specialists estimated the fleet has been reduced to five hundred million (one half of the original billion) and traveling at a slower rate of speed than before earth first engagement. Alexander give his second order to release, Operation Dragon." Operation Dragon are missiles all over the world, but have a shorter space travel range than the Titan longer range space missiles, the hundreds of thousands Dragon missiles all over the World pay load are the World's past Biological terror of the world such as anthrax, Ebola, Yellow Fever, and several more of the world once feared infections. Again, after six months, Supreme Commander Alexander tried to reason with the aliens and he received the same reply. Alexander issued order to launch all, "Operation Don't Breathe." For the first time, hundreds of thousands, "Black Flag." Missiles are hurtled in to outer space, each warhead carrying several tons of terrible weapons of war in their war heads, such as Muster Gas, Chorine Gas, Nerve Gas, and several other deadly gases. After two months, Alexander tried to reason with the potential invaders and their answer was the same-no negotiation.

CHAPTER 9

Aliens Sustain Great Losses

The fifth year was coming fast, the radar specialists have estimated that the once one billion space ships were down to thirty-five millions, five million ships per-continent still enough ships and probably enough storm troopers to conquer the world. Vice -President Stone and Sergeant Will tried to console the President by say that no disease, biological agent, gas, and chemical that you commanded to be deployed against the alien invaders are stronger than a cold to people on earth now. That is because earth people are survivalists and have somehow became immune to these past mass casualty producing weapons. All of a sudden, they saw the World Supreme Commander Alexander smile and commanded Stone to get him audience with the underground. Immediately, Stone left the Command Center. An Alarm went off; Alexander hurried to the control room in five minutes about thirty-five million space crafts will enter earth's skies. Alexander starts the count down, "five, four, three, two, one, zero," From the view screen of the Command Bunker all over the World the sky lit up from the firing of the alien invasion ships and after several hours the firing slowly ceased. Alexander carefully watched the monitor screen and when the space ships got within three hundred meters of the earth, Alexander gave the order for, Operation Let Loose." A hail of missiles, rockets, boulders, tree arrows, and stones, and other works of man's ingenuity came crushing into millions of the aliens' warships and in some cases crushing down on millions of the aliens' warships. By night fall the engagement slowed, there were only eight- space crafts flying, and five of them showed serious damage. "Operation Alien Defeat" was working, so far, there had not been any reports of injuries or loss of lives. Supreme Commander Alexander gave his radar and space specialists ordered to cut or end all possible space ships' communications with the Command ship, other space ships, and their planet by using Electronic and internet Warfare.

Stone came in the Command Center and Alexander asked, "Is it good news or bad news?" Stone informed Alexander that all the World underground leaders would like to meet him in a secret bunker in Jefferson City, Missouri. Immediately, Supreme World Commander Alexander said, "I will be ready to leave in two minutes. Sergeant Will, you will be in Charge of the Command Center and if Stone and I befall so deadly faith, you will assume President of the World Congress. Here is the code to our World Nuclear and Hydro Missiles Cache Number Ten; you will know what to do."

Within minutes, Stone and Alexander were on their way to Jefferson City, Missouri (with Missouri being known worldwide for their cave systems); it is not surprising that the meeting with our underground brothers and sisters would be in Missouri. While we were in a meeting with possible allies, the world guerilla and insurgency forces were having a field day with the alien storm troopers. Hundreds of thousands of alien storm troopers dismounted out of their aerial crafts along with thousands of light and heavy armor vehicles. The sophisticated tactical, trained, and heavily armed storm troopers were no match of the centuries old tactics and destructed power of people who knew the terrain and had fought several World Wars. All around the world starting at 0001 hour (one minute after midnight), guerilla and insurgency forces had been executing raids, ambushes, blowing up space ships, using fires to kill, maim, cripple, and mutilate the aliens. They have been blowing up convoys of alien vehicles, using hit and run tactics on units, shoot move and scoot methods to disorganize storm troopers' formations, blowing dams drowning hundreds of thousands of alien storm troopers. They killed alien storm troopers using booby traps, antipersonnel mines, destroying storm troopers' light and heavy tanks with tank mines, channeling light and heavy armed vehicles and storm troopers off cliff in rapid waters. Snipers were able to score many kills because the storm troopers moved in mass formations as in ancient, medieval, old world war, revolutionary war, and the American civil war maneuvers. Valley people using boomerang, slingshot, bow and arrows, hatches, axes, spears, rocks, and stones have been all effective weapons in killing alien personnel. With bridges collapsing with vehicles and troops on bridges, train loaded with explosion killing aliens and men dressed in well-camouflaged gillies suits killing alien storm troopers and their vehicles. They have been staying close to their down space crafts for protection and to reorganize and to consolidate and possible to prepare for another all out and desperate offensive or attack.

However, without the help and assistance of the underground forces, it be another past war situation, Alexander recalled reading about centuries ago a war called Vietnam. This war could last ten or more years with thousands of friendly casualties, both dead and serious injuries. When all the World underground leaders (more than half wore symbols from the Academy of Roughful Military Institute) were seated and they quickly gave allegiance to the World Congress and especially to legendary Commander Alexander. Supreme Commander Alexander found out that the underground allies represented tens of millions of people so numerous even their leaders in more than twenty years could not tell the true number of their command. The underground men, which represent tens of millions of people were well armed and trained. Once organized in two days, Supreme Commander gave the order to release, "Operation the Dogs of War," on the aliens. With the aliens not being able to rule the sky and limit aerial war ships, and storm troopers short on ammunitions; they were doom for defeat. The World for two days without breaks sent waves of F35s, A10s, AC130, A64s, bumblebees, B52s, and B51s. Huge armies surrounded the alien invaders and they attacked and attacked day and night until the alien forces were annihilated. Within two days, the war of the world was over. The alien's mighty billion space crafts' armada were down to one small space ship and five living aliens. One of the five alien survivors was the alien commander and though he was badly shot up,; he will live. He made a nonaggression treaty with President of the World Congress. Now working in the capacity of the President, Alexander had their one space ship fueled and supplied with enough provision to last them for the five years trip back to their planet and galaxy. The brightest and best scientists will study their technology and weapon systems if they break the treaty arrangement and attack earth in the future. The world will be better prepared to fight would be space invaders, other invading aliens of their kind, and possible other potentially lethal invaders or attackers.

CHAPTER 10

Five Aliens Go Home

When the five surviving aliens were loading, they could see watching them hundreds of thousands of well-armed Earth's soldiers. They were watching and in some faction daring them to come back to continue their feeble quest to conquer, enslave, and colonize the World's People. The President Alexander arranged this scene to convince the aliens that the earth was heavily populated and armed and breaking the treaty would be both foolish and disastrous to the aliens. It's just not going to happen and the people of the World want to guarantee it by studying and researching their technology and showing the alien a show of force—a tradition as old as warfare itself. The war machine (the world's people) of the world which surrounded the alien space ship know that the heat of combat has combined the World as one while in the past the World were thirty-two separate nations and a once hidden underground nations, now they are one. The electron and radar specialists have a view of the planet earth and a true picture of the size of the world's warriors and their war machines. But the aliens could not get a true glimpse of the size of the surrounding victorious army, but to them, it had to look masses thus sending the intended, disguised, and misleading message to the aliens and their commander that earth people are well armed and can protect the earth from any invasion from outer space. Nevertheless, they looked long and hard at the show of force and when they took off, they left like a bat released from hell. The advanced radars reported that they never slowed down and they were still traveling at light speed when the space ship vanished from the earth's radars range. The war with the aliens was over and the world had only one causality a computer personnel fell asleep at his desk. He fell over and he hit his head. He had to have stitches.

Supreme Commander Alexander had completed his destiny or had he. He had commanded a force of unquestionable size against a potentially unbeatable force. President Alexander and his wife will stay in the World Congress' Capitol and after ten years, Alexander retires. Alexander and his wife will live happily at the small manor; Mary left them. Their three boys (John, Stone, and Williams) will followed in their dad's footsteps.

For three years, Alexander and his family enjoyed the peaceful and comfort life of the island country. But today will bring another episode in Alexander's life, one because of Alexander's purpose and destiny, he can not escape. Occasionally, Sally and Alexander would go to the beach and they would watch the birds, boats, ships, and the waves of the ocean. Today seems as if it would be no different, except while Sally and Alexander sit peaceful on the rocks overlooking the ocean sceneries, Alexander hears noises behind his wife and him. He turns toward the noise and is not at all surprise to see in the distance the shadowy outline of two men walking in unison side by side in perfect step coming toward his wife and him. As they close, the distinct shape of two men dressed in black suits and wearing sunglasses become visible. He looks at Sally and she responds or answers without a single word, with no more than a single nod of approval, "Yes." Alexander reflects back in time and remember the first time; Mary and he met the two men dressed in black suits and wearing sunglasses and Mary signified approval with a single and simple nod giving approval to enter the fore coming adventure.

THE END

About the Author

Amond Williams lives in Frohna, a very small rural area in Perry County, Missouri. He graduated from Perryville High School on the thirty-first of May 1974. In 1973, Amond Williams, a high school senior, joined the army's Delayed Entry Program, and after graduation, on the fourteenth June 1974, he entered the army. After a little over two decades, Master Sergeant Williams retired from the army with an Honorable Discharge. Amond Williams has an associative degree from Pike Peaks Community College, Colorado Springs, Colorado, and a bachelor of science in social science teaching education (secondary education) from Fayetteville State University, North Carolina. Amond Williams has ambitions to attain a master's degree in education and write several other books. Though this book is definitely, Mr. Williams's first authorship work, he holds credit with several other authors, as SFC Amond Williams—Winning in the Jungle.